The Travail of Dieudonné

PEAK LIBRARY

Fictional Works

The Travail of Dieudonné

Francis B. Nyamnjoh

EAST AFRICAN EDUCATIONAL PUBLISHERS LTD.
Nairobi • Kampala • Dar es Salaam

Published by
East African Educational Publishers Ltd.
Brick Court, Mpaka Road/Woodvale Grove
Westlands, P.O. Box 45314
Nairobi - 00100
KENYA.
Email: eaep@eastafricanpublishers.com
Website: www.eastafricanpublishers.com

East African Educational Publishers Ltd.
P.O. Box 11542
Kampala
UGANDA.

Ujuzi Books Ltd.
P.O. Box 38260
Dar es Salaam
TANZANIA.

© Francis B. Nyamnjoh 2008

First published 2008

ISBN 978-9966-25- 557-0

CHAPTER ONE

The skies rumbled with thunder as a gust of wind swept past the struggling Dieudonné. It was pitch-dark and he was blinded by alcohol but the man's staggering steps were very sure. His pathway was a network of confusion but he had become an experienced mole. Many years of using the same footpath had imbued his legs with eyes of their own, enabling them to pick their way through the intriguing corners with bewitching ease and precision.

But Dieudonné was drunk – very drunk indeed. He staggered and groped on the dark pathway that meandered to his shack in the heart of the ghetto. Because he loved his drink, Dieudonné seldom came home sober – certainly not when he was financially viable, or in the company of the generous, or had a winning beer bottle cap, or when he would be allowed to drink on credit. Today, he was quite oblivious of the blood that oozed from his tiny, heavily scarred and shapeless legs. He couldn't even remember that he bruised them when he fell over one of the rough wooden benches in the popular Grand Canari Bar. He was drunk already, and the person who caused him to fall over had gone unpunished despite adding salt to injury by calling him 'vieil ivrogne' and 'espèce de sauvage'. Not that he would have done much anyway, for he was old and frail and knew himself well enough to avoid starting a scuffle he couldn't carry through. For one thing, he was much too tall and lean to win a fight against any of the more robust clientele of the Grand Canari, who were mostly from the forest areas where the climate, coupled with good food, yielded tougher body types. He coveted the youthful and energetic enthusiasm with which these tougher guys responded to the musical therapy daily served by the Grand Canari. But he hated the potent concoction of ecstasy that the musical frenzy blended with alcohol tended to yield in such muscular youthfulness. This was not the first time that alcohol had connived with external forces to make a chicken of him. If he could reflect, as he often did, he would recall numerous such instances over the years, from his own days of youthful exuberance and energy. Rogues had manhandled him countless times. More gifted disciples of the bottle had deceived him with Machiavellian ease. And he had been robbed of his source of daily happiness more times than he could recall. But as a committed drinker, Dieudonné knew that death alone stood in the way of his friendship with the bottle. He had grown to depend on the companionship that the bottle provided where human beings had failed him. It was simply too difficult for him to say no to the good feeling that alcohol provided. Nothing purified the soul better than a good drink well taken in good company.

The Grand Canari was a remarkable, gigantic triangular wooden building at the top of the hill that had served as a warehouse in the past when formal business used to thrive in this part of Nyamandem. Clients sat on benches and chairs around tables and away from a large circle at the middle reserved for dancing. The bar's doses of music, dished out in full blast by powerful loudspeakers, charmed clients from far and near, promising respite for all those who came to drown their problems in beer. Others came to wash in the particles of happiness that the winds of life in the city had blown their way. The bar's potholed floor told the story of its popularity with ordinary folks, and also of the energetic manner in which its numerous clients responded to the therapeutic potions it offered. To some, it was a ministry of enjoyment; to others a lot more. The bar offered everyone what they came to seek, and was respected for that. Its walls were covered with advertisements exalting the many wonders of the various brands of beer, ranging from the 'les moments forts' of the 'rafraichissante, intense, subtile, savoureuse et dynamique' 33 Export – 'the friend of friends', to the 'refreshingly smooth enigma of darkness' powered by Guinness, inviting customers to seize their life chances, through the 'refined and enlightening flavour' of Beaufort, 'the king of beers'. On bar walls as well, were carefully framed awards, collected over the years from the tens of breweries that competed for the attention of Grand Canari and its clients. Interspacing the framed awards were delicious witty quotes by famous people on the merits of drinking. Also on the wall, at the centre of everything, was the picture of President Longstay, beneath which was inscribed in bold blood-red letters: 'L'homme lion, l'homme des grandes ambitions'. Not comfortable in the company of a lion of such distinction, Madame Gazellia Mamelle, the proprietor – a veuve joyeuse and lioness in her own right – had taken the precaution of taking attention away from herself by not having her own picture on the walls of the bar. It was her civic duty to facilitate the ambitions of 'Le Guide Eclairé', The Enlightened Guide of Mimboland, albeit 'quelqu'un que Dieu a rejeté' or someone whom God rejected, as the records of the seminary where he had trained would bear out.

As Dieudonné made his way through the maze that was his neighbourhood, he thought of everything but the following day's work. Dieudonné worked for Monsieur and Madame Toubaaby, a middle-aged Muzungulander couple with an expensive residence at Beverly Hills, the exclusive exuberance of Nyamandem where, as it was rumoured, the stolen wealth that failed to make its way out of the country tended to be buried in extravagant luxuries that were simply out of this world. At Beverly Hills, passers-by were never tired of feeding their eyes with sights of wonderful white houses that looked like wedding cakes. It was where the nouveaux riches took refuge from the contagion of the nouveaux pauvres. He was used to his drinking mates referring to Beverly Hills as 'the poor man's idea of paradise'. Along with the rest of the poor, he wondered if religious leaders weren't in fact pulling their legs when they preached of a greater paradise hereafter.

Wouldn't it be more sensible to show people how to realise their dreams here and now? How could people confined to the margins cope with an idea of paradise that was greater than their most extravagant dreams, the rich man's mansions and effortless life at places like Beverly Hills? These were issues that he thought about and discussed with his friends in the warmth and friendship that only alcohol could offer. But when he lost sobriety, these preoccupations with poverty and misery sought refuge in his subconscious, giving way to a strange feeling of well-being, of freedom, and even of belonging.

Dieudonné's working day began at 7 am and ended at 4.30 pm, if he was lucky and his usually demanding employers pricked by guilt. As if to compensate, he was often late for work, but when he turned in to work later than 9 am, either Monsieur or Madame Toubaaby would come to fetch him in their senior executive Mercedes 280, their urban car, to distinguish it from Monsieur's pre-historic Land Rover, the bush car. Now Dieudonné was thinking neither of his job nor of his employers. He was thinking of nothing. He scarcely thought of a thing when he was drunk. Even Tsanga, his beloved wife, ceased to exist. All he would do instead was debate thoughtlessly with fellow drunks or whoever gave the impression of listening to him. He never felt bored when he was drunk; boring though he sometimes appeared to others. But once out of the bar, Dieudonné always tended to go homewards, even if he never actually arrived, as would happen occasionally.

The darkness seemed to thicken around Dieudonné as he staggered nearer his home. He fell again, as he usually did, abandoning himself to his sensitive wobbly legs. He had been very unfortunate that evening, and the darkness was actually making matters worse. In his senses, he would have marvelled at the amount of blood that oozed afresh from his renewed bruises! Enough to fill a bucket of Longstay's dripping ambitions! Yet he was quite unconscious, including even of his latest stumbles! Drunkenness gave him a certain kind of insensitivity. The next day, he would join his wife to marvel at the bruises on his tiny legs. Sometimes he was reluctant to admit Tsanga's accusation that he had answered nature's call in bed. That was always a most ridiculous moment, since they were a childless couple, and Tsanga seldom went out drinking as well. But whenever she did, she was sure to be forced to admit responsibility for the mess on the bed, even when the stench clearly emanated from within her husband's trousers! He was talkative, and had mastered the art of outtalking others, including his wife.

Dieudonné arrived home at last. He felt the door. It was locked. He gave it a rap. There was no answer. He knocked harder, still no answer. He banged at it frantically. A neighbour complained in broken Muzungulandish. Dieudonné ignored him and banged even harder. There was nothing the neighbours hadn't done to make him change his habits, but they had come to the conclusion that with him, drinking was a curse against which he wasn't capable of much. Dieudonné would have no neighbours if others had their way and if decent accommodation in the city was not so much beyond reach.

He kept banging. Perhaps Tsanga was not asleep. Perhaps she merely wanted him to use his thick skull. She knew that his key was with him, and that all he had to do was look in the only pocket of his trousers that had escaped the determined rats of the starved neighbourhood.

When the door refused to open in spite of all his efforts, Dieudonné gave up. He slumped across it, facing upwards like a dead man receiving his final visits before burial. Although the night was cold and it had started to rain, he fell asleep.

Tsanga heard him snore, and she knew immediately what had happened. She got out of bed, adjusted her wonder bra, tied her loincloth firmly round her rounded bottom and went to open the door.

"Poor thing," she sighed in Nkola, and carried her wet and enfeebled husband in, effortlessly. Although in the prime of her elderly years but younger than her husband, Tsanga was still incredibly energetic for her age, a fact Dieudonné was all too familiar with from her repeated complaints that he wasn't living up to his manhood. In frustration, she sometimes likened him to a soaked box of matches.

She peeled his clothes off, placed him on his side of the bed, and spread out the old blanket riddled with holes to cover him. Then sitting by her notorious husband, and unable to go back to sleep again for his snores and groans irritated her beyond measure, she nursed her wrath in preparation for attack at daybreak.

Tsanga had been forty-five when she married Dieudonné four years ago. He was her seventh husband. With him, she had decided to end her chequered love life and to settle down for good, although his drinking was often in the way of her expectations. Her past marriage life was rich and rare, a source of pride in a way, its sad moments notwithstanding. She came from a group where people cherished variety, inspired by the rich exuberance of their natural environment of rainforest. The reasoning was simple: If a balanced diet of food made for a healthy person, a balanced diet of partners made for a healthy love life. Had the ways of others not deformed their world, she would, instead of ending up with a poor, good-for-nothing weakling like Dieudonné, have married a tribal notable, a thoroughbred with a touch of class. But things had changed to the extent that the nobility and prominence of old no longer had a place in the limelight. Nowadays things scarcely ended up as well as they started off. She had loved and dumped men just as she had been loved and dumped by men. Tsanga often wondered whether she was the same woman who, as a young village girl, had sparked off duels among the truly virile of men. But life was full of contradictions, and she knew it just too well.

CHAPTER TWO

Tsanga was early to rise. It was Saturday and she wanted Dieudonné to be at Beverly Hills in time to start work at 7 am. She wished history would not repeat itself. Thinking of what happened a couple of weeks back, she muttered prayerful words of thanks to her God of the Catholic faith. No one would have convinced her that Dieudonné was going to escape dismissal when he stayed away from work on a Saturday. She looked again at her dead log of a husband. She was worried about the way he slept. It was normal for Dieudonné to talk when drunk, not sleep like a dead wood. She was impatient and afraid. She tried in vain to wake him up several times. Maybe an enemy had laced her husband's drink with poison, she thought. 'God forbid!' Tsanga extinguished the thought with an exclamation. But Dieudonné's seemingly comatose condition only intensified her fears and suspicions.

The Toubaabys were a couple that believed nothing must go wrong on Saturdays. They had the habit of inviting their friends over for meals on most Saturdays. For this reason, there was always extra cooking and cleaning for Dieudonné to do on this sacred day of the week. Monsieur and Madame Toubaaby were furious when Dieudonné failed to show up. Their indignation and disappointment made them feel like politicians manoeuvred out of office. And their fury only surged to fever pitch when they drove to Swine Quarter to fetch him but found neither him nor his wife at home. Tsanga had been very quick; she had rushed into the house and bolted her door immediately she caught sight of the Toubaabys approaching her house. The Toubaabys turned back infuriated while Dieudonné lay helplessly drunk inside the house, a piece of cloth tied round his mouth by Tsanga, to stop him from betraying himself by his senseless monologue, as was typical of him when he was drunk. The following day, Dieudonné had his subterfuge carefully prepared for him by Tsanga. On Monday, he told the Toubaabys of the sudden death of his sister-in-law, and how his wife and he had dashed to Nkola for the funeral. Most surprisingly, the Toubaabys not only fell for the story, they also sympathised with him. They even gave him a kilogramme of fish to cook for those who would stop by to sympathise with them. And so Dieudonné narrowly missed a confrontation with his strict no-nonsense employers.

Her wonder bra soaked, Tsanga tied her loincloth firmly over her breasts to stop them from dangling as she went about her chores. She washed her hands and face, and set about preparing breakfast. Then she decided she could wake her husband up in time for him not to get to work late. That would make Monsieur and Madame Toubaaby happy, and who knows what might follow? If Dieudonné could be punctual for a week or two, he might earn another gift of fish or something that would help to sustain life for a while. The financial drought was such that she just could not let such opportunities pass them by. Above all, folding her arms and watching her careless husband lose their only source of income was a luxury Tsanga could hardly afford.

She set aside several *batons des maniocs* and fried a cup of groundnuts, both to be eaten together with two avocados she had brought back from the village. Dieudonné's breakfast was usually heavy, because it was meant to serve as his lunch as well. The rats had helped themselves to the avocados, but there was still enough left to take her husband through his working day.

Though Tsanga was particularly conscientious, her husband was still fast asleep. Her numerous attempts to wake him up had failed. His hoarse snoring now put the croaking bullfrogs to shame. She was scared stiff. He had to wake up fast to have breakfast and get to work. The time advantage she thought he had was fast slipping away. She hated last-minute rushes, and soon, he would begin to race frantically in circles like an embattled cockroach.

She had to do more than wish he would wake up. She carried half a bucketful of water, moved across to the bed, and poured the water over her husband. That did not have any effect. His snores and groans continued unabated. What a deep sleep! Tsanga grew even more desperate. The thought that history could repeat itself almost drove her mad. This would mean a personal failure on her part. She would not sit and watch this happen.

Tsanga thought fast. She was desperate for a solution, and frightened by the prospect of the Toubaabys suddenly showing up to check on Dieudonné. How furious would they be to find their employee deep in slumber when he shouldn't be?

A bright idea struck her. She lifted Dieudonné out of bed and placed him on the cold floor, which, like the entire shack, was not cemented. Then she took the bottle of iodine, which the Toubaabys had presented him, and together with hot water, began to clean his bruises. That was just what was needed to rouse him from slumber. He screamed into consciousness. The iodine bit sharply into the thin layer of flesh that smeared his bony legs. This brought back a bad memory of his very first day with the Toubaabys, when he was attacked furiously by Flic, their merciless guard dog.

Dieudonné was stunned at the sight of his bruises. What had he done that his legs should look like that?

Tsanga would not answer any of his silly questions. All she said repeatedly was: "Dieudonné, you again are late for work. It might be the last straw this time." Her words, uttered in Nkola, sounded harsh and threatening.

Unable to elicit an answer from Tsanga, Dieudonné divined the reason behind his bruises, and what a right guess that was! From experience, he knew that alcohol was most certainly at the centre of the bruises. Aside from that, he felt generally weak, dizzy and thirsty. It takes alcohol to generate the craving for alcohol first thing in the morning.

Tsanga was soon through with dressing the bruises. Her husband was better late than never. But Dieudonné was quite incapable of helping himself. He could neither take his bath, nor eat his breakfast, nor go to work. He even refused to stir his brains up. All he felt was a dire need for a bottle of Beaufort, which he preferred to call King Size, and rarely, Chomeur, its other popular nickname. He felt he had to clear his head. In terms familiar to friends of the bottle, he needed a clearance.

At first Tsanga thought Dieudonné was joking, but when he insisted, she was infuriated. She began to scold, curse and invoke evil spirits upon him. She was angered by his downright display of childish irresponsibility. But, quite unperturbed, he turned a deaf ear to her ranting and raving. He only wished to be allowed to go back to sleep.

CHAPTER THREE

It was after 10 a.m. and Tsanga wondered why the Toubaabys had not yet called to inquire after their employee. This worried her even more. Perhaps they had made up their mind finally. And who would blame them? There was a limit to everything, tolerance and patience included. Dieudonné had surely exceeded his bounds, and would have to pay dearly for it. Tsanga felt hurt and abandoned. With a husband like Dieudonné, a woman was as secure as a single woman. His delinquency was disgusting. No sense of initiative whatsoever! As soft as ash! How did it ever surprise her that he still had not given her a baby to carry! Her anger and disappointment surged. Now that the Toubaabys had certainly said enough was enough, she wondered what Dieudonné was going to do. Poor thing, how would he come out of this? How was he to feed his appetites? She sighed in resignation. She allowed him to get back to bed. Even as a drunk, he would know she tried her best.

Indeed, Tsanga had tried her very best for Dieudonné. It wasn't easy to marry a man who had so little to offer, especially for a woman whose life had attracted men of quality and social standing. But life is life, and decisions are not always informed by logic and the obvious. Tsanga had married Dieudonné in her lowest moment of vulnerability. She had just left her sixth husband, a restless, stunted fat trader with crooked teeth and undersized lips, averagely rich but terribly ambitious, from the eastern grassfields of Mimboland, who had, in addition to treating her as an object, proved to be a sorcerer in several respects. First, Tankap, as he was called, given his aspirations to father money, had the unusual habit of tearing off pieces of her old clothes and using these to tie his money for safekeeping as he hated having anything to do with the bank. Second, he would shave off portions of her pubic hair when she was fast asleep, which he would use in mysterious ways, in the company of his mysterious friends with whom he shared a common ambition of greedy achievements in superabundance. When Tsanga became suspicious and asked him why he did what he did, why he wasn't using his own old clothes or his own pubic hair, he would mumble something unconvincing like, "You are my wife. You are the mother of my money." How could she mother his money when he was always accusing her of chasing away money by spending without relenting? He would say: "Money has no time to rest in this house"; "This house offers no refuge to money"; "You are so unkind to money. You hardly ever invite it to sit down for a cup of tea".

Worried, Tsanga had solicited the help of a diviner, the most respected of them in Nyamandem, a powerful marabout at the Muslim residential zone of the city, who was renowned for using Koranic verses to read the present and foretell the future, and whom rumour – a most privileged medium – held was regularly consulted even by the topmost politicians and intellectuals of the city. Upon seeing Tsanga, even before she had opened her mouth, the diviner had said, "I see trouble hanging over you like a swarm of bees. There is a one-armed man, short, thick and dark, with big evil eyes in a sinister room hungry for blood and human flesh. Whoever he is, run before it is too late. He doesn't mean well." Tsanga saw Tankap clearly from the marabout's description. Impressed but frightened, she paid the diviner and left in a haste, desperate to keep running until she felt safe.

She had reached home running, collected her belongings in a hurry, and sent urgent word to her 17-year-old son and only child, Atangana, who was making ends meet as *un débrouillard sauveteur* at the Sawang seaport, to keep away at all costs from his stepfather. But, as she was later to find out that same day, it was too late to save her son. Tankap had made a meal of the young man with his sorcery even before she started running, as news reached her late in the evening that Atangana had drowned mysteriously. It wasn't Tankap who reported Atangana's drowning. He couldn't be bothered. Instead, he had proceeded, without Tsanga's knowledge (not that she knew much about his shady business dealings) to inaugurate a bakery he had just acquired using fake banknotes from a certain Monsieur Nupieds, a Muzungulander (known in official circles as 'a career criminal') who was neck-deep in financial crisis and was liquidating all he owned to pay off his debts and avoid imprisonment for fraud or to pay his way out if imprisoned. For, as one notorious armed robber once declared to a journalist who wanted to know why he never served his prison terms, "on achète de tout dans nos prisons, même le droit de ne pas y rester" – one buys all in our prisons, even the right not to stay there.

Had Tsanga known what others knew about Tankap, she would have done all not to marry him. For, what was there to be got from a husband who was so greedy that he would crush with his teeth a fly that had fallen into his drinking glass, saying, "That should teach the likes of you not to dare to want to share my beer"? A man who was ready to wake the dead up and even to follow them to the world hereafter to honour their debts, but who was never in a hurry himself to honour his own debts? "Qu'il se reveille. Qu'il m'envoie d'abord mon argent. L'homme ne peut pas changer le destin de l'autre," he would say of a debtor whose death had just been announced. Tsanga had not heard the story, until it was too late, of how Tankap and two business associates had agreed to pay MIM$10,000 each in honour of a business partner that had died suddenly. The two others had kept their word by placing MIM$20,000 in cash in the coffin bearing the dead man. When it was his turn, Tankap mumbled something about not having cash on him, signed a cheque for MIM$30,000 to the order of the dead man, pocketed the MIM$20,000 left by the two others, and sealed the coffin. She had not known either that Tankap allegedly rejoiced when his left arm was chopped off in an accident, because he thought that having one arm only would discourage family and friends from always expecting him to dip his hands into his pockets. Tsanga most certainly would not have dared, if she had heard what everyone else knew, the real reason Tankap's first wife had fled him. A reckless Pajero-crate had knocked down one of Tankap's twin boys. Terribly sorry, the Pajero-crate had offered Tankap MIM$40,000 to rush his son to hospital, only to be flabbergasted when Tankap pleaded with him to knock down the other boy and pay for it as well. His wife did not stay another minute when the story reached her; she collected her boys and fled for dear life. Only a perfect stranger like Tsanga could have married a dangerous man like Tankap. The excitement of their first date had probably blinded Tsanga to the possibility that Tankap could be up to no good when her body was all on fire, not because he had brought the woman out of her, but because he had carelessly handled her without washing his hands after eating roasted meat dipped in extra hot chilli powder. If only Tsanga had known all these things about her would-be husband, she would have kept her distance, and Atangana just might have lived.

Tsanga had wept and wept for her beloved Atangana, and had been literally drifting when she came by the Grand Canari Bar, her first time ever, and decided to get in and contemplate her life and next move. Badly needing solace, the loud music of familiar Bikutsi tunes from her very own village of Nkola attracted her to the bar, where she met Dieudonné for the first time. It was his extra vulnerability, his lower than low, that captured her attention, and made her respond positively to his dramatic and ludicrous proclamation of love.

"Je m'appelle Dieudonné", she could still hear his first words ringing in her ear, as he screamed at the top of his voice to stay above the boom of the music and competing din. After which he had proceeded to declare his love in a style of his own.

He had told her: "Beauty, you are pretty. Will you make my day? I have nothing to offer but poverty, guaranteed. But I promise you won't regret a thing. Je suis très riche en amour."

Smiling, she had replied: "Dieu m'a donné un mari." And more to herself than to him, she had added: "I have seen worse." As an experienced woman, Tsanga had come to know that it was good to be cheap from time to time for the sake of the poor who could not buy up and the rich who loved buying down.

Things had moved fast. They had gone to see her parents at Nkola, who though reluctant to demand payment of a bride price from a son-in-law that could barely feed their daughter, had wished them luck. Moreover, they were quite frankly sick and tired of having to refund bride prices, of hardly benefiting from the expectation that 'the mother-in-law's basket is never full', and of not being able to be accused of 'an in-law who visits forever ends up being fed a chicken smaller than a bird', given Tsanga's high turnover of husbands. With their daughter's bride price, they had learnt to behave like the servant in the Biblical parable who was too suspicious to invest the money his master had left with him, and who had proceeded to dig a hole and bury the money to await the master's return, sure of having the last laugh. So Dieudonné was doubly blessed, first by his chronic poverty, and second by the lesson Tsanga's parents had learnt from her six previous marriages, about most of which Tsanga hardly spoke openly with him. She mentioned most frequently the sixth husband whom he had succeeded to know, and about whom he was bound to hear, given that their first meeting was the very day she left him in disastrous circumstances. The only other husband she mentioned regularly was her late son's father, her first love – 'l'homme qui m'avait decapsuleé' – whom she married briefly in her village years, but which marriage dissolved shortly after they moved to

15

the city. They had gone into a bar one day, and he had felt terribly jealous that a total stranger had gazed longingly at her and had offered her a drink, which she had accepted. And when she had dared to tell him that she felt he was greatly underestimating the size of her heart, as it had room enough even for ten loves and more, his anger had hit the roof. He had denounced her there and then, had stormed out, returned to the village and held her parents hostage until they had coughed up the goats and fowls he had paid for "their prostitute of a daughter".

With these memories, the best Tsanga's parents could do was wish their new son-in-law volumes of luck. "So long as you are happy together, we are going to be happy. Tsanga is our daughter. She has spoken well of you. She says you saved her from suicide, for which we are grateful. If she has chosen you with her heart, she will find a place in there to make you happy. If it is one of those illnesses that make women of the city restless, forgive our daughter, and we hope you'd understand we meant well." To show Dieudonné they meant well, they had given Tsanga, to cook for her husband, lots of bushmeat parcelled out from the baboons, chimpanzees, gorillas and monkeys that her father regularly hunted for his clients to feed the rich and hungry of Nyamandem.

And with her parents' blessings and caution, both Tsanga and Dieudonné had returned to Nyamandem, determined to make the best of their marriage.

CHAPTER FOUR

When Dieudonné awoke late in the early hours of the afternoon, there was no trace of Tsanga. Her dresses had vanished with her. His age-old utensils smeared with Muzungulander colonial history in Warzone and Mimboland, and his only chair worth the name, an invaluable present from a priest – one of scores of former employers – were nowhere to be found. Dieudonné looked under the grass mattress of his bed. The money he had hidden there was gone. So was his hope of ever returning to Warzone. He collapsed over the bed and began to weep, not for anything material, but for the loss of the company of the woman he believed loved him as much as he did her, even if she had often criticised him for not being man enough.

Dieudonné wept like a child forsaken by a foster mother. He sat by the gate of the elaborately fenced compound of Monsieur and Madame Toubaaby. His white shirt and khaki brown shorts were filthy. He had not washed them for weeks, despite the fact that the Toubaabys insisted on neatness as a requirement for serving as a houseboy. His black sandals were dirty, and his white socks had turned brown. The blood clots on his legs were evidence that he had not taken a bath for days. As he wept, some of his tears washed away some of the blood clots, making his wounds look like a commentary on his failures to tame his appetites.

Both Monsieur and Madame Toubaaby were in, busy at their books as usual. Known jokingly among their students as 'Monsieur et Madame Ethnologie', they were members of the association of Muzungulander intellectuals referred to as 'Les Facilitateurs', and lecturers at the University of Asieyam, 'la machine à fabrication des chomeurs', the factory for churning out the jobless. Dieudonné knew the couple to his fingertips, crooked and tortured by chores though the fingers were. He knew them to be principled, a quality they had demonstrated repeatedly. They had insisted, for instance, that he dress like a schoolboy and relate to them as schoolmasters, in order to qualify to be termed 'houseboy'. It would take some convincing for them to alter their minds. But somehow Dieudonné felt hopeful. He wished for sympathy and salvation, Insha'Allah. To him, the Toubaabys had sanctioned him beyond the bounds of severity. Not to pay him for one whole month was simply too harsh a punishment. And what had happened to all his years of dedicated service?

Why did they ignore the story he told them about Tsanga? Did they really mean it when they claimed it was none of their business what happened to him or his wife? Yet they had believed when he lied to them not so long ago about her losing a sister. What had happened between then and now that they had resolved not to know anything about him outside the confines of their secluded residence? Did they really think that he was worth his job as houseboy and cook for pets, and nothing more? What had become of the little acts of kindness that he had grown to expect even from a selfish couple like them?

He remembered his father's early years as apprentice weaver in Warzone and shook his head in self-pity. Then things weren't the way they were with him today. For one thing, life was cheap as value was measured in chicken and ordinary transactions done in eggs. And masters were generous by instinct. The Toubaabys were being bizarre. As learner-weaver, Dieudonné's father not only used to be paid a wage, he was treated above all as an integral member of the family of his master. Dieudonné could reconcile nothing. It was simply queer for the Toubaabys to treat him like a lifeless tool, a machine of sorts that relieved Madame of her housewife chores, a zombie. He was bitter and sad. He was still weeping and muttering when the gate bell rang. He hesitated for a while, before deciding against opening it. It rang a second and third time. At the fourth time Monsieur Toubaaby came rushing. He was an exceedingly tall man, and for a while towered over the tall Dieudonné, staring down on his grey hair. This made Dieudonné feel the weight of the injustice even more.

"How many times have I told you to open the gate when someone rings?" asked Monsieur Toubaaby, his hand unconsciously contemplating his baldness.

"But you have also told me to hesitate if I don't know who rings," Dieudonné challenged. Then quickly added, still in tears, "I was hesitating, Monsieur."

"Go to the store and fetch what you have to prepare as food for the animals. Make sure you remember to clean them after their meal. Thorough cleaning is what I mean, not anything done in a hurry or with a grudge. We've told you that you can jolly well resign if you consider our sanctions too severe! After all, Nyamandem is crowded with hundreds of thousands seeking employment as domestics!"

Dieudonné was startled by Monsieur Toubaaby's screaming tone. As he struggled down the steps leading to the store, which was situated just behind the elegant main building, Monsieur Toubaaby unbolted the gate to let in his visitor. He must have had foreknowledge of the visit, for he didn't ask his usual question: "c'est qui?"

"Ah, c'est vous Dieumerci? Welcome."

"Good morning, Professor. I had some problems finding the right bus, so I couldn't come as early as we agreed," Dieumerci, a young man of average height and size, fair in complexion, with a beardy pimpled face, apologised, flashing his eyes around, in admiration of the richness of the surroundings. The compound was striking with exuberance and splendour – a beautiful lawn, immaculate flowers, and light blurbs on trees and hedges, everywhere. The electric fence alone must have cost a fortune, he thought. All through the bus ride to the Toubaabys, he had commented within himself how filthy rich Beverly Hills and its occupants were. He noticed tall, exuberant electric-fenced villas glittering with wealth and protected with iron gates marked *'Interdiction Formelle de Franchir la Barrière de Sécurité/Chien Mechant/Mbwa Mkali'*. To have so many broad streets, all well tarred, in a city overburdened with potholes, was, to say the least, to be filthy rich and damn lucky. To have electricity enough to forget switching off the streetlights at dawn in a city where everyone else suffered repeated power cuts was to be filthy rich and irresponsible. Every comfort in Beverly Hills seemed exaggerated in its superabundance, just like misery, the lot of most of the rest, was overly present in the bleeding ghetto Dieumerci was coming from. Either God had been waylaid, attacked and all his generosity stolen at Beverly Hills, or his sense of creative balance had fled him altogether when it came to deciding what to make of Beverly Hills. Dieumerci had gathered that mostly foreigners and a handful of distinguished nationals inhabited the possibilities of this sumptuous residential paradise. This degree of splendour, Dieumerci would never have associated with Monsieur Toubaaby, who always came to the university in a Land Rover that looked like an archaeological resurrection of a pre-historic technology. He would never have thought that Monsieur Toubaaby, a critical academic, belonged with the privileged few bent on riding "big tough Mercedes and sports cars that fly over the potholes of Nyamandem", to quote a nosy journalist jailed recently for his "daring pieces" in a paper the high and mighty love to hate, and above all, for refusing to let his conscience be bought with brown envelopes.

"Never mind, Dieumerci. Come along with me. The books are ready for you there at the store. I took them out from my study last night." Monsieur Toubaaby's Tougalish was as good as his Muzungulandish, though Dieumerci couldn't detect the accent that tended to corrupt the Tougalish, because he wasn't exceptionally good at it either. But Monsieur Toubaaby preferred to speak Tougalish to Dieumerci, who was more articulate in it than in Muzungulandish.

They both went down to the store where Dieudonné was busy defrosting and removing scales from fish. Monsieur Toubaaby indicated the pile of books on the table to Dieumerci, who was preparing a mini-dissertation for an honours degree in social history.

"The only condition I pose is that you have to read all those volumes on the spot," he told Dieumerci jealously for the fifth time in three days. "Do not take home any, whatsoever," he reiterated.

Dieumerci hesitated for a moment.

"Do you understand?" Monsieur Toubaaby glared into Dieumerci's eyes as if the latter was guilty already. The sight of his eyes through his thick glasses frightened Dieumerci.

"I do Professor," Dieumerci whispered.

"You can send for me in case you don't understand something, or would like us to have a brief discussion."

"I am very grateful, Monsieur," said Dieumerci. "I will let you know as soon as I run into difficulties," he added, smiling his appreciation, but somehow feeling guilty for failing to be respectful by addressing his tutor as "Monsieur" in place of "Professor".

Monsieur Toubaaby left the store and Dieumerci settled down on the volumes. He looked forward to devouring them, one and all, in Tougalish or Muzungulandish. He would love to be professor and fountain of knowledge just like Monsieur Toubaaby. Though this was still a long way to come, it however remained his dream. He had shortened his daily prayers to merely asking God to arm him with courage and intelligence, which he repeated ad nauseam.

Once he had settled down, Dieumerci got immersed in the books. In fact, he was so absorbed by his reading that he forgot to get acquainted with the curious-looking elderly man. So he was angry with himself when he raised his head only to realise that it was lunchtime, and he had to hurry back to the Restaurant Universitaire for a meal of imported trotters and Muzungu-Avenir couscous. The professor showed him to the gate and bid him goodbye. He would call again the following day.

"As long as you're not earlier than 8 am," the professor reiterated, and bolted the gate after him. Then he turned to go back to the house to join Madame Toubaaby, who was almost out of patience waiting for him at the dining table.

As Dieumerci walked away, he could hear Monsieur Toubaaby asking the elderly man if the animals had been fed yet. Who was this curious elderly man named Dieudonné? Why did he dress himself up as a schoolboy to cook for animals? And what special animals were these that had a cook? There was a lot more than books, which he would have to know at the Toubaabys, Dieumerci promised himself. He would have to read with his eyes and ears wide open.

CHAPTER FIVE

The following day Dieumerci was at the gate at 8 o'clock. He was even earlier than the elderly man. Monsieur Toubaaby and his wife were still having breakfast but he was not angered by Dieumerci's promptness. He interrupted his breakfast to open the gate and unlock the store – a gesture which didn't leave the observant young man unimpressed. Monsieur Toubaaby went back to finish his breakfast. Ten minutes later, he returned to attend to Dieumerci. A real academic jackass, thought Dieumerci, wondering just how many of such people there were at the University of Asieyam, where the ambitions of the belly were rumoured to have corrupted the integrity of the intellect. The belly had become the main intellectual compass around campus, where scholars eager for integrity and excellence were sure to end up either in prison or in the wastepaper basket of the system, in tune with the policy of 'pourbellisation des intellectuels radicaux'. This had resulted in a university littered with what the critical philosophy Professor F.U. Iroko, a rare exception on the scholarly landscape, had termed "shoe-shiner, slash-and-burn, one-legged intellectuals", earning himself the status of persona non grata among his peers. To live a life that was completely dedicated to scholarship wasn't within the range of most so-called academics of the belly with intellects 'diluted by too much beer' or rendered infertile by the largesse of the truly powerful. Not when shortcuts to fame remained as tempting as they were numerous. In most courses, it was normal for late-coming students to be told: "You've gained a lot by not being here to miss nothing," by fellow students bored stiff of 'les intellectuels du ventre stérile'. Ailing, salary-starved lecturers charged students exorbitantly for notes that were already out of date when they themselves were students decades ago. Dieumerci remembered how recently an underpaid and underfed lecturer, flat as a leaf, twice encircled by his belt, and wearing a T-shirt that read: 'You Are Lost', was giving a talk on 'The Future of Africa', when he was rudely interrupted by angry students swearing: 'Find yourself first!'

"Is there any problem, Dieumerci?" Monsieur Toubaaby sat down beside the student, his glasses delicately balanced on the tip of his pointed nose. "Know that I'm entirely at your disposal," he added.

"No, Professor, not yet. So far there is no major problem, because all I did yesterday was to go through the tables of contents of the books. It's today that I intend to start the actual research," replied Dieumerci, as guilty as the student that he was.

"You must bear in mind that you are entirely free to recast the formulation and conceptual framework of your research to suit your facts. Remember that the test of the theoretical pudding is in the practical eating. Instead of: *'Cotton Production and Economic Alienation in Warzone During Muzungulander Colonial Rule,'* you might end up with something like: *'Cotton: A Paradox in Warzone'*. You should read everything critically, taking nothing for granted. In social research, nothing is too sacred to be questioned. That is what writing a mini-dissertation is all about, creating something new through constant and critical interrogation of received wisdom. You must avoid always looking down like a pig. Try to look up at the sun and around; you would be amazed by what you read or are told. It's essential to avoid being *un cochon académique*." He paused, took off his glasses and started to clean them with a soft tissue taken from the front pocket of the jeans shirt he was wearing.

"In the absence of any questions," he began, leaving his seat, "I take leave of you. Make yourself at home and good luck," he added with a broad smile.

Monsieur Toubaaby left the room, repeating: "Question, question, question … that's the mark of a good scholar."

Dieumerci felt relieved when Monsieur Toubaaby finally turned his back. In his mind, the professor was guilty of repetition ad nauseam – "I'm not thick. He's been telling me the same thing for three years! He keeps shouting: '*Apprendre pour comprendre pour reprendre*' as if in mimicry to Auguste Comte's famous: '*Savior pour prevoir pour pouvoir*'." He laughed to himself and muttered, "Nutty, nutty professor."

A few metres away he met Dieudonné, who had just arrived. The two men exchanged greetings. Or rather, the servant greeted and the master answered reluctantly. Just then, Madame Toubaaby came out. Dieudonné turned round and whispered a polite "Bonjour Madame".

"Bonjour," she replied impatiently. "You still have the clothes you washed last time, to iron before you start cooking for my darlings, n'est-ce pas?" Then with a smile of benevolence: "And today you can have a free meal here if you do your work well and timely, n'est-ce pas?" Madame Toubaaby expected Dieudonné to be pleased with the rare offer, especially as the word 'free' did not appeal to her, if it meant losing ground or losing grip.

"Oui, Madame, d'accord. I'll do my very best," Dieudonné replied politely.

Madame Toubaaby didn't get the enthusiastic response she expected, but she was in no mood to prolong her encounter with this silly fool who never ceased to make an issue of his age. She had warned him repeatedly against such disrespectful conduct, such as him avoiding work by claiming that: "An old man must never be in a hurry as bearer of wisdom, as he just might fall short of it." She had made him understand that what you get is what you work, and did not hesitate to deduct and deduct until his thick skull had got the message.

She went into the house again, followed closely by her husband, who reminded Dieudonné to clear the breakfast table ensuring, as always, that the leftovers were carefully parcelled and stored away.

Dieudonné made his way down to the store, counting the stairs like a blind man, his mind pregnant with woes. He wasn't surprised to find Dieumerci, to whom he said "Bonjour mon fils", as if in compensation for the son he had always wanted but never had. He must be a polite boy, not the arrogant type that wouldn't hesitate to spit on the face of an elderly person. Dieudonné assessed from the way Dieumerci answered his greetings.

Dieumerci looked up and could read from the old man's eyes that this was a weak and harmless man, the sort created as pawns to be used and dumped. His father had taught him from childhood how to distinguish the sheep from the wolves, just by looking at a person's face.

"I apologise for failing to introduce myself yesterday," Dieumerci confessed, turning to face Dieudonné, who was preparing part of the broad table to start ironing a huge pile of clothes.

"I think you were rather too involved with the books," said Dieudonné. "But I understood perfectly. Every other student that has been here before you has always been amazed by the volumes placed at their disposal. I imagine it was the same with you yesterday, am I right?" he asked, beginning to iron the first dress. To Dieumerci's ear, his Muzungulandish sounded like the delicious broken version he was used to among illiterate plantation workers from West Mimboland.

"Yes, that is what happened, in fact," admitted Dieumerci. "This is actually the first time I have seen an individual who owns so many books on a single branch of knowledge. I can't imagine how big his entire library must be!"

Dieudonné laughed a brief laugh of superiority. "Have you ever been to the coastal region of West Mimboland?" he asked, interrupting the ironing for a while to sprinkle a bit of water on a dress that he considered too dry.

"Yes," Dieumerci was wondering what Dieudonné was up to.

"Then you can understand if I compare his pile of books to Mount Mimboland," said Dieudonné, resuming the ironing.

"Yes?" Dieumerci was amused by Dieudonné's sense of exaggeration. This certainly was a most exciting old man, he thought, pleased to know that his reading at the Toubaabys was not going to be as boring as he had feared. Dieudonné was certainly the man to chat with during breaks.

Dieudonné recounted what he once overheard Monsieur Toubaaby telling a Mimbolander colleague from the same department where he taught. "If I am an academic polygamist," Mr Toubaaby had started, referring to the fact that he was multidisciplinary and broad in his reading, "it is in compensation for my having failed to become a polygamist in real life." Then he had rushed to add that it wasn't so much his failure as the fact that his culture did not tolerate the pleasures of it. "So the only theatre left for me to operate my polygamy is in academics," he had concluded, giving his colleague enough to chew, as female university students equally offered those in need an opportunity to catch up on the delights of polygamy.

"Does it surprise you?" asked Dieudonné, unable to suppress a chuckle himself. "Why, when a Muzungulander decides to study books, he eats and sleeps books, he breathes books, he celebrates books. His isn't merely touch and go as is typical of some of us in black man kontri. What I've described is only Monsieur's bookstore, which does not include Madame's. Hers is equally a marvel. A second Mount Mimboland, with her choicest being books on cats and dogs," he added with a chuckle. "Dem get book plenty pass how graffi chief get woman and pikin. And dem drink book like man pikin drink mimbo, je te jure." He spiced it up with Pidgin, determined to pass Mr and Mrs Toubaaby off as a couple glued to books and paper from dawn to dusk.

Dieumerci was immediately attracted by the old man's sense of humour. The apparent ease with which Dieudonné switched from Muzungulandish to Pidgin, or mixed both languages, won his admiration. 'A real linguistic blender', he thought.

"I wonder if they ever consult all the books in their possession," said Dieumerci, dog-earing a page he didn't want to miss.

Dieudonné cleared his throat and laughed like the possessor of superior knowledge that he certainly was.

"They are as busy as soldier ants," he told Dieumerci. "In the morning they rise at 7 o'clock, never later. They bathe themselves and eat their breakfast, and are ready to tackle their book-work by 8 am, when they start biting into volume after volume, biting without blowing. I pity the books. They work on their books till 9 pm, barely interrupting themselves at 12.30 pm and 6.30 pm to lunch and supper. They go out only when they must, which is when they have some shopping to do, lectures to deliver at the university or very intimate friends to visit, who incidentally are just a handful. As a matter of principle, they never leave this compound when neither the night watchman nor I is here. In fact, they are like bees, either flying protectively around their hives, or sucking much needed nectar out of plants. I haven't been here late enough to know when they go to bed, but I don't think they sleep earlier than midnight. And I wouldn't even call what they do sleep. It's more like an opportunity for the mind to go hunting for new ideas or new ways of reading and writing their books. Some weeks ago, I overheard a concerned visitor ask Madame Toubaaby: 'When do you rest?' To whom she replied: 'When I'm working. Work is less tiring than idleness.' Amazing! "

"One might have thought that as the rich couple that they are, the Toubaabys would spend their time eating delicacies, drinking rare wines, and travelling round and taking the whole wide world in photographs. Isn't it so Dieudonné?" Dieumerci pronounced the elderly man's name with care and respect for age.

"Who told you my name?" Dieudonné feigned surprise, smiling satisfaction. "Man no di know."

"Can anyone say how many times a day your name is pronounced by the Toubaabys?" Dieumerci was getting more and more thrilled by Dieudonné's humour. "And, with both our names rooted in God, how would a name like yours escape me even if mentioned in a whisper?"

For a minute or so Dieudonné focused his attention and skill on a pair of trousers whose delicate material made it susceptible to undesired twists and folds. It was something he detested in ironing, because Monsieur Toubaaby was extra concerned about "le pantalon de ma veste en laine", as he chose to call it. This was a suit that he never wore, unless as member of jury in a thesis defence at the university. When he had passed the test, Dieudonné again divided his attention between ironing and Dieumerci, who had seized the opportunity to read the page he dog-eared.

"You say me and you be God namesake, which God be you? Won't you tell me à qui j'ai affaire? Perhaps you want me to offer you a bribe of kola nut or cigarette?" Dieudonné gave Dieumerci a friendly tap on the shoulder.

"I'm neither as demanding as a mange-mille nor as thirsty as a civil servant. I'm a mere student who needs no bribe of kola nuts and who happens not to be a smoker. My name is Dieumerci Aphrika, and I come from the Wami highlands of the forgotten West."

"Thank Papa God. But why the forgotten West?" Dieudonné asked with a smile, as if he knew the answer to his own question, which he did. Just the other day at the Grand Canari, he overheard a disillusioned civil servant from the Wami highlands complaining bitterly how nothing had changed in his daily life since President Longstay came to power. The man, who was half drunk, did not like the fact that irregular salaries had forced him into farming coffee and cocoa that did not yield much. He said he had never imagined himself handling a hoe one day, but today, 'it is thanks to the hoe that I am still alive.' He swore, if only his vote could count, never again to vote for President Longstay, for: "We no longer have the means to feed our children and grandchildren, to send them to school, or to attend to their health needs." And he couldn't understand why they had been abandoned to themselves when they had clearly been told that with the coming of Longstay to power, "things were going to change". He called for a messiah with the exclamation: "Our situation is very critical! Nous vivons une terre des mots pas une terre des miracles – We live a world of words not a world of miracles". And a warning: "If you want a goat to remain on its rope, make sure the grass around it is green". So, Dieudonné did know the answer to his own question.

But Dieumerci, not aware of this, answered. "Because the only time government remembers my people is when there are false promises to make, taxes to collect, or electoral votes to ignore. As such, we are what you may call *small die fowl*, meant to be fed upon in chicken parlours by privileged others who, while having reason to claim *suffer don finish*, compel the rest of us always to keep in mind that the end is far from near: *suffer dey front*. As such, we live the silent fears of the *sans domiciles fixes*."

Impressed by Dieumerci's play on SDF, the newly launched Social Democratic Front opposition party in the highlands, Dieudonné said: "My child, I like the way you talk. But you are still a student. I wish you were a man of experience, and still spoke the way you do. For who can tell the gender of a child that is still in the womb?"

Dieudonné paused and stared at Dieumerci for a while, tears in his eyes. "Dieumerci," the elderly man burst out, his voice gentle and firm, "I wish it were possible for you to remain the student that you are. As such, you would be avoiding one or two things. You would avoid contamination by the rest of us, or contaminating those around you." The elderly man looked so depressed, all of a sudden, as he struggled to dry his tears with the back of his hand.

Dieumerci was touched. "Why do you say that, Pa'a Dieudonné? What happened to the happiness that was engraved on your face a while ago?" He could see a man fighting desperately to be happy, but not always winning.

"There are moments like this when sadness and bitter memories suddenly take hold of me. This happens when someone or something reminds me of my turbulent and miserable past. Sometimes it just comes. You haven't had lots of bad experiences, have you? May Allah protect and preserve you. I've had all sorts of experiences – a few happy ones, but mostly sad, soul-rending experiences that are better forgotten. But how can I avoid memories over which I have so little control? Just how can I shut this mysterious gateway into a past that beckons and lures the present to see in it the way to the future? How I wish I could do the impossible!" Tears fell on the dress he was ironing, and he placed the hot iron over the wet spot to dry. He wiped his eyes and cleared his nostrils with his hands, which he rubbed on his shorts. He turned to Dieumerci who was saying something.

"May I know of these experiences whose memories sadden you so?" Dieumerci sounded as sympathetic as he ought to be.

"I'm an old man, and my experiences are as grey as my hair," replied Dieudonné, aged more by poverty than by years. He ran his hand through his hair, and pulling at random, cut some off to show Dieumerci. They both laughed.

"My experiences are life-long and bitter," he went on. Dieumerci listened with keen interest. "But I can't tell you for two reasons. First, though I've seen you twice, I don't know you yet. I know you are Dieumerci, a student of my master. That's all. But should that be all? I have to know you more if I must tell you the story of my life. The world is full of smiling faces, but who can say for sure with faces? Could you, just by looking at their smiling faces, say who, of Musa or Hassan, is for war, and who for peace; who for life or who for death?"

Dieumerci shook his head in denial. It was impossible to say who stood for peace and life or for war and death in Warzone just by looking at the faces of the leaders of the different factions. But why did Dieudonné tumble on Warzone as an example? What had he to do with Warzone? Dieumerci wondered, but Dieudonné didn't give him the chance to wonder aloud.

"Second," Dieudonné went on, "apart from the fact that there is so much work here for me to do, I'll never tell you my life story at the residence of people who, like their predecessors, saw no better place for me than under their feet. To tell you anything serious here would be like burying a baby's umbilical cord in a foreign land. If you really want to know about me, I can either tell you the story at my place, at yours, or at any other place we agree upon, Insha'Allah. But certainly not here."

"That's okay with me," said Dieumerci. "I agree that you've known me for two days only, but given your experience, you can determine whether I'm someone to be trusted or not. With no intention to blow my own trumpet, I can assure you that I've been brought up in a rigid traditional setting where respect for one's elders and cultural values are essential ingredients for one's social and mental health. So, take my word." He sounded academic, but Dieudonné was used to academics. What would they offer if he denied them their stock in trade?

"I know, I see."

"What part of Mimboland do you come from?" Dieumerci inquired, still trying to solve the puzzle of the Warzone example.

"That's a question you should have asked a long time ago, isn't it?" Dieudonné stared at Dieumerci.

"I realise that, and I apologise," said Dieumerci, full of guilt.

"Never mind," Dieudonné reassured. "Hasn't Monsieur told you that I'm not a Mimbolander? Hasn't he mentioned that I'm from Warzone?"

"Warzone!" shouted Dieumerci, all excited. "Did you say Warzone?" He sounded like one who had heard the unexpected, pleasantly.

"Yes, why?" Dieudonné couldn't divine what the hell the matter with coming from Warzone was. People came from Warzone every day, every hour, every minute! The whole region was flooded with refugees from damned Warzone!! He stared at Dieumerci in utter bewilderment.

"I'm sorry if I've surprised you," Dieumerci apologised. "But I'm so pleased to learn that you're from Warzone. The piece of work I plan to write for my degree is to be on cotton production in Warzone," he explained, still excited.

Dieumerci was deeply pleased to learn of Dieudonné's Warzoner origin. He was suddenly optimistic that an opportunity had at last presented itself for him to compare what the books said with the opinions of someone who perhaps might have experienced colonial cotton farming, or who at least, had known people that did. Though he knew nothing yet about Dieudonné's past, Dieumerci was very hopeful that his mini-dissertation would read much better, thanks to the additional ingredients Dieudonné was likely to provide. He was just too aware of the fact that most studies never penetrated deep enough into the real issues they claimed to deal with. They tended to be of a touch-and-go superficial nature. To dangle at the mouth of knowledge, as it were.

Dieudonné's story would be most timely for nearly all of the knowledge Dieumerci possessed on Warzone was about her post-colonial situation, which wasn't exactly what he wanted for his mini-dissertation. He knew for instance that Warzone was granted independence in 1960, but what did he know about the whole period of colonial rule from 1900 to 1960? Nothing. Dieudonné would have to tell him what the peasant's life was like during this earlier period, and perhaps how cotton farming was introduced – cotton which today was responsible for more than 70 per cent of Warzone's foreign earnings. Dieumerci also knew about the war that was raging, and that was costing the country much in human life and in resources. "A bleeding catalogue of carnage, impunity and indifference", an embittered journalist had described Warzone recently. Yes, Dieumerci knew of this war of greed that had turned thousands of innocent children into soldiers, drug addicts, rapists and butchers. He knew of thousands of Warzoner refugees who were scattered all over Africa, fleeing the mayhem fuelled by Muzungulander merchants of death through local warring lords and pied pipers of baby soldiers. But what did he know about the causes of the war, apart from the fact that iron ore, diamonds, uranium and the likelihood of huge deposits of oil were the motive behind intervention by ruthless, conniving and competing foreign interests?

Dieumerci was clearly excited. He wished Dieudonné could stop the ironing and tell his story there and then. There was much he wanted to know about Dieudonné the person. His ethnic origin, to start with. Was Dieudonné an Arab from the north or was he a native African from the South? What did he worship: the Muslim Allah, the Christian God, the God of his Ancestors or a buffer of all three Gods? Had he in his youth by any chance met Allakuhbat, Warzone's first president who was ousted in a coup? How much of Soule's rise and fall from grace could he remember? What did he know about Sulaiman and Abdou? Did he agree with those who criticised Musa for being a stooge to Muzungu-Avenir's Amadou Kano, or with those who claimed that Hassan was receiving tuition from Muzunguland on how to be a good Muslim? Did he have any ideas of his own as far as the factional war in his country was concerned? And, last but not least, was he in line with those who argued that the real reason for the fighting was the question of who should control the cotton plantations of Warzone, as well as the diamond, iron ore and uranium deposits in the so-called Eldorado Oasis? Did he know more than was rumoured that huge deposits of oil had brought the Muzungulander sniffing aggressively for opportunities? And selling the same weapons to the warring factions as if in the hope of inheriting the wealth of the land when the sons and daughters of the soil have all perished? Did he support foreign intervention in any form or for any reason? And what did he think of the heavy toll of a war whose head or tail not even the lords of war that fed it could tell? A war that had funnelled hundreds of thousands of Muzungulander weaponry, wreaking havoc and cheapening life, killing children, raping women to death, chopping arms, maiming villagers, making millions homeless, and ravaging hope.

All these were some of the things Dieumerci hoped to find out from Dieudonné. He just couldn't wait to hear the story. But at the same time, he had to be careful not to give Dieudonné the impression that he was merely interested in his own personal gain. He didn't want to pass for a journalist who would stop at nothing to harvest a good story. Dieumerci knew well enough how people hate to be used by others. However, he wanted to fix a date with Dieudonné when they could meet and have a long conversation together.

With the zeal and anxiety of a child on a hard-earned birthday party, Dieumerci couldn't wait. "Pa'a Dieudonné," he began timidly, "I'd like us to arrange when and where to meet and get to know each other better. Don't you think?"

Dieudonné hesitated. "Let me think about it." He was cautious, and rightly so, for Mimboland had the reputation of a country où on ne sais jamais à qui on a affaire, where keeping up appearances was the order of the day.

But Dieumerci was insistent, like a child with whom the word 'No' did not exist.

Dieudonné could see that Dieumerci had the tenacity of a tick. Reluctantly and with a smile, he conceded. "Can you read till 4.30 p.m. when I knock off, Insha'Allah? If you are ready to wait for that long, then we can go home together to my place. Once you know where I live, we can meet much more easily to decide where and when to meet again for the conversation." Dieudonné yielded, inspecting a dress he'd just finished ironing. Madame Toubaaby would shout warm urine out of him if something were the matter with her white dress!

"I agree. Thank you. Thank you very much," Dieumerci replied with haste and enthusiasm, as if he feared Dieudonné might reverse his decision.

"*Hakuna matata*," Dieudonné said, showing off a popular Swahili expression he had picked up, and continued to iron Madame Toubaaby's delicate silk blouse. "Truth is sweet. Even a liar knows that," he said, as if addressing the iron in his hand.

Dieumerci went back to his books where he soon buried his attention. He had to make sure there were questions to ask when Professor Toubaaby came round again, seeking intellectual stimulation. To tell the Professor again that he had nothing to discuss would be a clear sign that he was definitely not a serious student. In short, that he was *un cochon académique*.

On his part Dieudonné soon finished ironing and left the store for the kitchen where he began to prepare lunch for Madame Toubaaby's eight cats and a dog. It was two hours to lunchtime, and Dieudonné had to beat the clock to win the meal that Madame had promised him. His mouth watered as he thought of the delicious meal, which was most likely to be the leftovers of what Monsieur and Madame were going to have for lunch. You couldn't get luckier as a houseboy. How blest must Dieudonné have thought himself that afternoon! But the unfortunate fact that Tsanga, his wife, had deserted him stole away much of his delight, and made him look like the forlorn orphan that he was.

Dieumerci settled down with *The Call of the Dark Continent* by Walker of the Wesleyan Methodist Missionary Society. Monsieur Toubaaby had recommended Chapter VII strongly, in case Dieumerci intended to make religion a factor in understanding cotton production in Warzone. It was curious that in West and Sahara Africa, Islam, not Christianity, had succeeded best, and quite curiously as well, Muzungulander values were least entrenched in this part of the continent. Although repulsively prejudiced and overbearing in tone, the book made some very interesting observations, which Dieumerci did not hesitate to note.

Walker dismissed the 'pagan' ways of Africa as 'doomed and ready to pass away', as they were clearly not rooted in any civilisation worth writing home about. If there was anything to worry about, it was Islam, 'by far the most terrible external foe that has ever opposed the Church of Christ' – 'a direct challenge to the Kingdom of Christ' and contender against Christianity for the possession of Africa and the world. To Walker, the popularity of Islam came from its endorsement of the magic, witchcraft and superstitions of the Africans. Instead of awakening the intelligence of Africans 'to see the folly and uselessness' of such superstitions, and to lead them to put their confidence in God, Islam had only added new superstitions, new chains, thereby giving its authority to many pagan ideas and practices. 'The Koran itself is degraded into an instrument of magic. Portions of it are sewn up in leather pouches and worn as amulets; phrases are written on pieces of board, and the water used in washing off the ink is swallowed as medicine'. Because 'The Muslim missionary asks very little of his converts', because he neither insists on 'change of heart or manner of life', nor on 'baptism unto repentance and the remission of sins', it is a lot easier for Africans to become Muslims than it is to be Christians. 'In a word, Islam in Africa checks no vice and denounces no errors but superimposes the all-powerful name of Allah on the superstition which it finds and gives the dignity of a world-religion to unwashed heathenism.' In the face of such concessions by easy-going Islam, Christianity is severely handicapped. 'The messenger of Jesus cannot descend to the methods of his Muslim rival; he cannot marry into a pagan family; he cannot lure the superstitious people with Christian "charms"; he cannot accommodate his Gospel to the low and degraded impulses and instincts of the heathen. Such considerations may well discourage. They suggest that the tide of Islam cannot be stemmed.'

Recalling Monsieur Toubaaby's famous adage 'the test of the theoretical pudding is in the practical eating', Dieumerci wondered why in Warzone where Christianity had met with minimal success, cotton farming introduced by Christians seemed to thrive. If economy had a direct link to religion, one would expect Christian economies to fare less where Islam had succeeded, and vice versa. Dieumerci wasn't sure this was the situation with Warzone. Unless, of course, the success story of cotton could be traced to the regions of Warzone where Christianity was relatively better implanted than Islam! He would have to take a closer look at the economic map of the country.

Dieumerci read over the notes he had made to ensure that he had taken them down properly. Walker's observations about the different fortunes of Islam and Christianity made perfect sense. A religion that sets out not only to convert souls but also to change a people's culture, traditions and ways of seeing, thinking and doing, is bound at best to be related to as a cosmetic external to one's essence, or at worst toyed with and dumped. For a religion to be truly meaningful, its God ought to be accommodating, not domesticating, negotiating, not imposing. Dieumerci was firmly convinced about this, and could see why Christianity would either adapt or perish in Africa.

He put the book aside and took up another, one on cotton farming in Warzone by a Muzungulander economist, Jean-Pierre Goutier, which he read and summarised the main arguments from. The book, although largely uncritical of the Muzunguland practice of subsidizing its own farmers while underpaying African farmers, contained very useful statistics on cotton price manipulation by Muzungulander traders to pay less and earn more, which he would certainly treat himself to in writing up his mini-dissertation.

At 1.00 p.m., Dieumerci could study no further. He was tired and famished. He didn't breakfast in the morning because he expected to return to the Restaurant Universitaire for lunch. He hadn't anticipated the development with Dieudonné, and even when he agreed to stay till 4.30 p.m. he had hoped that the Toubaabys might invite him to lunch. But what happened took him quite by surprise. When his discussion with Monsieur Toubaaby was over, the latter went in for lunch without inviting him, without even finding out whether or not he was hungry. He knew of none of his relations or friends who would behave in a similar manner, not even to a perfect stranger. Unable to bear the hunger and annoyance, Dieumerci asked Dieudonné to postpone their appointment. He rushed over to the university restaurant, still puzzled by the snobbery of his favourite professor.

CHAPTER SIX

Dieudonné pushed over the only chair in the room for Dieumerci in a gesture of courtesy. It fell over. The two legs that had supported the rest of the frame for this long gave way. It was as if it had connived with Tsanga to do him in.

"Man no die, man no rotten," Dieudonné sighed in resignation. "Dieumerci, you see for yourself how poor my place is. Apart from the overly creviced and crumbling walls, which make it easy for mice and cockroaches to rush in and out as they like in search of what is not there, I don't even have a chair you can sit on."

There was a lot less to the room than met the eye.

Dieumerci shook his head with understanding, as Dieudonné continued to confess.

"So it's not convenient for us to work here. I, therefore, suggest that we move to your place, unless that is too far away. In which case, I would say we sit at the Grand Canari Bar a couple of streets up the road, at Le-carrefour-de-la-joie, where most people go to feel good. If, of course, you have a little money to loosen my tongue. Comme disent les Mimbolandais de l'ouest, 'small no be sick. Cow wey yi no get tail na God di driv'am fly.' I talk best when I am lubricated, Dieu est grand." Dieudonné spoke a jerky mixture of Muzungulandish and Pidgin.

"I know that the Toubaabys don't need your services on Sundays, which means that you are quite free today. But my place is near the university campus, which is very far from here, as you probably know," said Dieumerci. Then he hesitated, wondering if Le-carrefour-de-la-joie was indeed the right place to go, given what he had heard of the place as a market for cheap joy, cheap friendship, cheap sex and cheap violence, where drunken nuisances were fetched in vomit-smeared wheelbarrows and dumped in smelling gutters of standing urine-water and rotting refuse. At Le-carrefour-de-la-joie, thieves were known to be faster than a plane taking off, and unsuspecting passers-by were raided, stripped of valuables, and even the pockets of their underwear turned inside out within seconds of setting foot there. Thick, muscular and aggressive '*Njambo*' and '*débrouillard sauveteur*' youth were there to finish off the job of dispossession by luring passers-by to embrace the illusion of winning millions playing poker and other games of chance. With the words 'Qui remet à demain trouveras malheur en chemin', they made gamblers of everyone with something to lose. And the forces of law and order had become champions of such lawlessness and disorder. Increasingly, Mimbolanders were giving up on the police. 'Take them to the police? You are not serious! As soon as you turn your back, the police will take money and free them, and before you know it they are drinking with you in the bar and threatening to deal with you', Dieumerci recalled a man who had seen it all recently laughing off a journalist on FM Mimbo who wanted to know why more and more people at Le-carrefour-de-la-joie resorted to beating and lynching those they caught or suspected of stealing. 'I'll never go to the police again. They arm and encourage these thieves, they are all thieves,' the man had insisted. Instinctively though, Dieumerci knew that Dieudonné would tell his story better in the bar.

The very first time that they met at the Toubaabys over a week ago, Dieumerci had known there and then that Dieudonné was faithful to Bacchus. That first day, Dieudonné did have bloodshot eyes, and his breath did smell strongly, like the breath of a man 'qui se livre à la boisson mains et pieds liés.'

"I think we should go to the Grand Canari at Le-carrefour-de-la-joie instead, provided we aren't disturbed there," said Dieumerci, as he pulled his purse out of his pocket to examine its meagre contents.

"There is no cause for concern," Dieudonné reassured, not financially, of course. "The population at Grand Canari is always scanty on Sunday mornings. Although it shares Le-carrefour-de-la-joie of Swine Quarter with several other bars – Travail-Avant-Tout, Elise Bar, Eldorado, Maison Blanche, Gentil Bar, Super Pakita, TamTam Weekend, Marché Mondial, Lefam-So, Sauvateur Bar, Rêve-d'or, Amical des Soûlards, Des Noctambules, Des Ça Gâte, and Le Mimboman – the Grand Canari is an exceptionally friendly place, quite generous to the likes of me. Unlike other bars where there is unnecessary trouble making, breaking bottles and fighting with broken bottles, at the Grand Canari I feel completely at ease, as its other customers are generally unassuming. It's a jolly bar, the one and only. I think you are going to like the atmosphere," he sounded confident, like one who knew everything about his favourite bar.

Dieumerci had that I-will-see-before-I-believe look, but went along.

The two men picked their way through the muddy road that meandered through rows of dilapidated shacks, accompanied by Prince Eyango's music that was blasting away from the neighbourhood. Both hummed along, with Dieudonné even singing along in sections. The bit he particularly liked was that of a man steeped in poverty and misery, resisting death. 'If you want to die,' the man tells his friend, 'take at least a glass of Gold Fasse before you die. And when you get to hell, tell my elder brother that I have problems but I refuse to die. My problems are not mine alone to carry. So why worry? Même si les poches sont troués, je suis toujours en veste et cravate …. A chacun son problème…'

"Do you mind if we walk a little slowly," Dieudonné was panting. "My legs are not as nimble as yours."

Dieumerci apologised and slowed down.

It took them over half an hour to get to the Grand Canari, which was by the side of the battered car-infested Acacia Road.

Dieudonné and Dieumerci waited for another quarter of an hour for the overflowing traffic, with its thick dark smoke of pollution, to subside. They then raced across to the Grand Canari, gasping for breath.

Though Dieumerci knew next to nothing about road construction, he felt that circulation would be much easier in less narrow streets. But he had never seen a less narrow street in his life! Whether such streets existed elsewhere, it was hard to say. The streets in this busy but forgotten part of Nyamandem were not much bigger than the footpaths in his home village. And to make matters worse, the panting cars emitted smoke like the rainforest ablaze.

Dieudonné was right: there were very few people at the Grand Canari when they arrived. Apart from Precious, the young, pretty, delightful bubbly barmaid in spicy dress whom the male clientele stubbornly insisted on calling 'Le Barman', only four men and a woman were present. They sipped from their drinking glasses, chatted and laughed leisurely. Dieumerci, like a typical Mimbolander man, remarked – not without surprise – that the woman was drinking beer. Dieudonné was more used to beer-drinking women, seeing that he met them almost on a daily basis.

Dieudonné greeted everyone, who shook hands with him and called him a couple of nicknames. He appeared to like the names, and for some time exchanged jokes and laughed with the group. Then he introduced Dieumerci as a student and friend of "mon patron, Monsieur Toubaaby". The men were pleased and invited both to join them on the long bench. Dieudonné received his first gift of beer from one of the men – Chopngomna, a tall, dark and imposing man in a blue kaftan who was known in familiar beer circles as 'Le Bao' short for 'Baobab inderacinable', and who earned his living as a cashier at the state treasury of the fourth administrative district of Nyamandem, where he was 'Bonbon

Alcoolisé' or 'Joli Bébé' to the aspiring girls of a nearby high school, 'Moni Man Chop Fine Ting' to others who could only admire him from a distance, and 'Cow With Four Stomachs' to men who felt stunted by him. To older women here and there competing without much success for his undivided attention, Chopngomna was simply 'un vrai bandit comblé des conneries'. He owned two mobile phones – the latest, cutest and most expensive Nokia and Samsung in town; phones endowed with the fanciest ring tones that made him a popular spectacle around Nyamandem.

Dieudonné's favourite beer, King Size, was advertised as 'Mimboland's favourite beer', as 'a premium quality beer, genuinely fresh with a rich smooth, deeply, satisfying taste with millions of sparkling bubbles' and as 'a beer with which there is never a dull moment'. His love was deep for this light, tasty, well-balanced beer with a wonderful flowery aroma which he preferred *bien glacée*, regardless of the time of day. He examined the beer closely against the light. Satisfied that there were no sediments, he asked Precious to uncap it, which she did – with the loud pop of a fired gun – using a carved wooden opener the shape of a man's genitals popularly known as 'l'increvable ouvre-bière mimbolandais'. The beer foamed over, a sign that Precious had shaken it before opening. She apologised and, turning his glass horizontally, poured the beer gently down the side to avoid it foaming over again. Dieudonné took a sip, swirled it around in his mouth and nodded his satisfaction with the mouth-feel and flavour of his trusted King Size. He gulped and exclaimed: "Dieu est grand!" With the look of a well-travelled man on his face, he added, "King Size is like the River Nile. Once you have drunk from it, you will return to drink again and again."

What he appreciated most in his King Size was the aftertaste that lingered in his mouth after every gulp. The brewers of King Size had maintained the quality, taste, texture, aroma, freshness and filling quality of the beer over the years despite the generally fluctuating standards of brewing in the country and in spite of the threat posed by the repressive heat and sunshine of Mimboland. The brewers had invested remarkably in the interest of standards, passing from wooden beer kegs to stainless steel kegs, and supplying – at great discounts – refrigerators and coolers to big and serious clients like Madame Gazellia Mamelle of Grand Canari.

Dieudonné thanked Chopngomna, the man who loved playing word games with the names of drinks, and who had only one insult when drunk of his favourite Baobab, although never admitting ever getting drunk: 'De qui te moques-tu? You' face long like horse yi uwn. You' face flat like tyre for motor wey yi don burs'! Je mange le fruit de la sueur de mon front. Lock you' doti mop!'

Dieumerci asked for a Guinness – which Chopngomna said stood for 'goût unique des individus nés nobles et sans souci', but which he had heard others claim meant 'girls under immaturity never never enjoy serious sex' after the same Chopngomna had ridiculed him into abandoning his original option – Fanta, described mockingly by Chopngomna as 'fantastic Ashawo never takes alcohol'. Not wanting to pass for a prostitute, fantastic or not, Dieumerci yielded to the prejudice that any sweet drink was nothing but water, which made a man's stomach swell with urine, forcing him to visit the urinal every too often: 'drink'am go piss'. The second prejudice was worse – the implication that men only drank soft when they were taking treatment for venereal disease: Maladie D'amour. "La Bière c'est pour les hommes, les sucreries sont pour les femmes et les enfants", Dieumerci was told by Chopngomna in civil service Muzungulandish, a message Dieudonné translated into Pidgin to drive the point home: "Man pikin mimbo na for man pikin dem, woman mimbo na for woman and pikin dem."

As if to prove the point, Dieudonné soon emptied his bottle in a manly manner, warming up animatedly to Pierre Tchana's famous 'Il n'est jamais trop tard', which Precious had turned on as more clients trickled in.

Dieumerci was stunned by the speed with which Dieudonné emptied his bottle. He looked at the empty bottle, which was twice as big as his, and shook his head disapprovingly. At this rate, he wondered if Dieudonné would tell him anything intelligible. But the others who knew Dieudonné well merely laughed and made allusions to "Munding Swine Quarter". Dieudonné responded to this thus: "Oui, oui, c'est ça! Elle vaut de l'or!" There was every indication that these men enjoyed Dieudonné's company. Dieudonné, they said, was warm and full of fun. He must really have been funny, for everything he said elicited laughter.

"Give a man a fish and feed him for a day. Teach a man to fish and he will sit in a boat all day and drink beer," Dieudonné volunteered a fisherman's joke he had picked up from one of his Muzungulander employers.

His audience applauded, with some calling him 'l'indomtable Dieudonné'.

Chopngomna, with the bleeding wallet, offered Dieudonné two more bottles of Beaufort bien glacée. He also offered a round to those who took up his challenge to say as many times, and as fast as possible, the words: 'I want one White Horse'. As for himself, Chopngomna ordered another Baobab which he preferred to drink directly from the bottle, held at the neck.

"You di talk like sey you no di talk wey you di t-a-l-k," Precious told Dieudonné, as she uncapped his beer.

Looking at a disturbed Dieumerci, Dieudonné said, "Si tu veux que la chance te sourit, saisis-la – If you want luck to smile on you, snatch it." Then turning to his bottle, he exclaimed with total satisfaction: "King Size, l'équilibre parfait entre puissance et douceur! That is, the perfect balance between power and smoothness!"

"Les actions valent mieux que les paroles, action speaks louder than words," Chopngomna interjected, sipping his Baobab.

It wasn't until he had consumed the second bottle that Dieudonné felt his tongue loosened enough. He became increasingly talkative and, in a loud voice, promised everyone the story of his life. Dieumerci sharpened his ears and listened, forgot his Guinness temporarily, sat upright, and turned towards Dieudonné. The music was loud, but he was determined not to miss a word of what Dieudonné had to say, so he moved closer, knowing that it would be rude to seek to impose his will by asking Precious 'le barman' to turn it off or lower the volume.

"None of you knows the story of my life," Dieudonné began, still shaking to the music. "Some of you think you know me, but only I know the story of my life," he belched.

"Today you are privileged to know some of it. At least, what I can remember in a bar. I'll tell it to the hearing of this young and learned son of mine," he pointed at Dieumerci, "with the hope that he might write it down some day, Insha'Allah, so that posterity might also know about those of us whom history books and writers constantly fail to mention, because they have never bothered to see us as flesh and blood." He paused to gulp the third bottle of King Size. Then he asked, "Should I proceed?"

"Not before you are supplied with another bottle of Munding Swine Quarter," said Chopngomna, the cheerful giver of the group. "Les actions valent mieux que les paroles," he added.

To the offer, Dieudonné stood up and wriggled to Franco's 'Mario', which was now playing, and to which an albino gentleman in flowery attire sandwiched by two beautiful plump ladies dressed in colourful airy kabas were dancing expressively at the centre of the bar. The albino was known around as 'Bonblanc Mukala Ni-Ni', signifying 'Ni noir, Ni blanc'. He and his women were sucking whisky from sachets as they danced, the type drinkers had nicknamed 'whisky condom', because the sachets looked like condoms. Thinking of himself as a better dancer, Dieudonné almost asked the albino who was dancing with legs ajar: 'How you di dance like say you shithole di hala with pepper?' Fortunately he did not, for Bonblanc Mukala Ni-Ni was known to sting like a wasp.

"Yes, it's Munding," Dieudonné replied to Chopngomna, at the same time as he tried to sing along with Franco. "That is why I can drink many bottles without the risk of getting drunk. Beaufort is truly water as you say, Chopngomna," he told the cheerful giver, who himself preferred Gold Harp, known to him and his bar circles as 'government officers like drinking heavily after receiving pay', and 'get one lady daily, have another reserved permanently'. Regaining his seat, he added: "But I like Beaufort because it is the oldest beer around, the grandfather of all beers! Nobi our combi dem for church di call'am 'our daily bread' and dem de prayer 'Papa God for giv'am Beaufort today and forever and ever, amen?' I started to drink it a very long time ago," he added. "Okay, no palaver," he said to Chopngomna. "I'll have as many daily breads as you are ready to offer. I thank you very much, and above all, I thank Papa God for little mercies." Dieudonné was humble and cheerful in his thanks.

Precious brought the beer and uncapped it, then poured some of it into Dieudonné's empty glass.

"Mon soleil d'Afrique, mon jus de passion, sans conservateur, sans colorant, sans arômes artificiels," said Dieudonné with a laugh, meaning: 'My African sun, my passion fruit, no preservatives, no additives, no artificial flavourings.' He sipped from his bottle, leaving Dieumerci guessing whether the compliment was for the beer or for Precious.

As Precious returned to the bar, Dieumerci, who was clearly most anxious to hear the life story of Dieudonné, pleaded with her to lower the volume of the music so the conversation could flow audibly. She did and he smiled his appreciation, which she noted. Every other thing, including the drinking, which stimulated Dieudonné's sense of narration, was secondary as far as Dieumerci was concerned. He wanted nothing to stand in the way once Dieudonné began telling his story. Dieumerci turned to Dieudonné and said, "And you may proceed, Pa'a Dieudonné."

"Is that everyone's opinion?" asked Dieudonné, passing an inflated pair of eyes round the bar. The size of his bloodshot eyes caused all to laugh. Someone offered him a lobe of kola, which he thankfully threw into the back of his mouth where his teeth were still intact. "Kola nuts go hand in hand with beer, they make drinking complete," he commented and crushed, looking up. "I hope no one is surprised I can still crush something," he added, laughing as he chewed, recalling his father's 'soldiers are like horses; they must have good teeth'. As the son of a soldier, he added: "Even if I were to lose all my teeth, my jaws are so strong I could even bite a crocodile. My other bits may have gone into premature retirement, but do not underestimate my jaws."

Everyone laughed. A second person tendered Dieudonné a Bitter Kola, which he turned down, saying: "Démarreur? Pas pour moi. I have nothing to kick-start." He turned to Dieumerci, who accepted a Bitter Kola and added mischievously, "Give that to the Guinness drinker. Nobi I hear sey Guinness and bitter kola na hélélé for kick-start?" The bar reverberated with laughter at Dieumerci's expense as people savoured Dieudonné's aphrodisiac insinuations.

"Start the night with a Guinness," someone recalled a popular advertisement.

"There is greatness in every drop," another added.

"Nothing tastes like greatness," Chopngomna laughed deeply.

"Together with Bitter Kola, Guinness keeps the night awake," affirmed yet another man.

"Na number one carpenter for waist," a woman testified in jest. In his embarrassment Dieumerci did not notice when Precious winked with reassuring curiosity.

When the laughter subsided, Dieudonné looked in the direction of Chopngomna for his cue.

"You may go right on with your story," said Margarita, the ebony dark woman with prominent eyes, and a distinctly beautiful hairdo achieved by artfully weaving together her bleached natural hair with long attachments, probably harvested from a Muzungulander blonde. She had until then said nothing but giggled self-consciously, drinking Amstel, what Chopngomna preferred to call 'aime-moi si tu es libre', but which she, when she wanted to hurt him, would say stood for 'all major state treasurers embezzle lots'. Margarita was one of the more regular girlfriends to Chopngomna. He was married but could hardly be found in public in the company of the woman he was fond of calling 'my sweetheart of yesteryears'. To everyone who wanted to make him feel guilty as an MBA – Married But Available – he had this to say: 'Ce n'est pas que j'aimes tromper ma femme, mais il m'arrive de me tromper de femme.' – It isn't that I like to cheat on my wife, but it happens that I mistake women.

Margarita asked Precious to turn the music off completely. The colourful Bonblanc Mukala Ni-Ni and his well-rounded women, who were dancing, sat down reluctantly when the music died down following Margarita's point that it was still too young in the day for music and dancing. After insulting Precious for yielding too easily to Margarita, Bonblanc Mukala Ni-Ni ordered more sachets of Nikkita, their favourite from an avalanche of new vodkas, brandies, rums and whiskies in sachets that came under the name 'whisky condom', together with Cassanova, a red wine nicknamed 'Follow-me-to-cry-die' that tasted better mixed with spirits, and that in connivance with his women, played games with his sensitive anatomy. Generous to both his drink and his women, Bonblanc Mukala Ni-Ni impersonated at the same time the hoarse voice of the man in the radio ad inviting people to go for: 'Affordable delights without the pitfalls. Get a whisky. Get a condom. Drink more. Spend less.'

Dieumerci was grateful to Margarita for asking that the music be turned off, and thus suppressed the comment he was dying to make about her wig – "I've always thought that those who wear wigs can play lice a lot of tricks" – not knowing how she would take it.

Dieudonné cleared his throat and drained the lump with what remained in his glass. His lips were coloured red by the kola he had just eaten. He began his story: "I want to drown all my troubles, but have chosen beer, since we live so far away from the sea ..."

CHAPTER SEVEN

"Man yi kontri na man yi kontri!" exclaimed Dieudonné. "Qui est le type qui a chanté 'no condition is permanent'?"

"Isn't it Tchana Pierre, the Salsa King of Mimboland?"

"No! It's Manu Dibango, the King of Soul Makossa!"

"No make erreur! Na Sam Fan Thomas, Auteur for Makassi!"

"Tala André-Marie, you thick head!! Le Roi du Bendskin give chop for masa, masa like you. C'est lui! …"

"C'est Prince Nico Mbarga, Père for *Sweet Mother*, I no go forget you."

"How can you say that? Isn't it Lapiro de Mbanga, l'homme de petit peuple, le president des sauveteurs, whose music is like fire in the backside of big men? Listen to his *no make erreur, mimba we* and *surface de reparation*? He is the one! Those are his words … 'No condition is permanent. Bring me mbutu. Chop ma mop, suck ma tong, lick ma lips – show yi!'"

"I would have sworn it is Petit Pays, l'homme pimenté qui pique comme un avocat defenseur des femmes. L'homme pour qui là où il n'y a pas de danger, il n'y a pas de plaisir, the man for whom where there is no danger there is no pleasure."

"Non, non, non ! C'est Sustain Parole, l'auteur composateur *d'Aratatata chop die… fait moi bien.*"

"Aren't you all making a mistake? C'est le même type qui a chanté – God make man, man make woman, woman make Satan and Satan spoil the world."

"Non, non, non ! C'est Joli Bébé ! Man for 'L'amour n'as pas de compteur, love does not have a meter, who sings 'Tell a woman the truth she thinks it is a lie, but when you tell her a lie, she takes it for the truth. If you reveal your secret to a woman, know that you have given the key to your house to a thief.' It is he who sang 'no condition is permanent'."

"Typical of men isn't it? Bébé Mbonbolono is the name, the golden voice of modern Makossa. She, with the magic recipe for holding onto a man who won't stay, and how to get rid of a man who won't go."

"Correction sister … you mean Anne-Marie Ndze, Queen Mother of Bikutsi? Or is it Sally Nyollo, l'ambassadrice du genre?"

"Nonsense! Wrong, wrong, wrong ... everyone wrong …!" screamed Chopngomna, faithful to Tchana Pierre.

"Je te jure …" protested Margarita, convinced of Bébé Mbonbolono, in her famous song: 'Quelqu'un ne peut pas être quelqu'un sans son quelqu'un quelque part… No one can be someone without her someone somewhere.'

The audience competed for the right to be right.

"It doesn't matter, mes frères, mes soeurs, ma combi dem," Dieudonné regained captaincy. "I asked only to say the words of that song depict my situation. He sings, "Nobody knows tomorrow. No condition is permanent. Quand quelqu'un vous ferme ses portes, il faut le laisser en paix … Man yi kontri na man yi kontri", and captures both my missing home and hoping for home. Which brings me to the story of my roots. But first, let me kiss my King Size …"

His audience laughed as he gulped … belched … gulped … belched… murmuring: "Chérie, l'amour de ma vie".

"I'm a Warzoner, and not a Mimbolander from the North as almost everyone around here thinks. I was born in a little village near Warzone City. Not being of noble birth, my father earned his living as a weaver. He wove mats, which he sold to fellow Warzoners of Arab and non-Arab origin, and to foreigners from all over Africa. His mats were of high quality, and our family was able to live a good life by selling them, since everyone by custom needed a mat of their own. It is a curse to rely permanently on the mats of others. In those days, one didn't need the same amount of money as we do nowadays to live well. Things were a lot easier. In his early years, my father didn't need money to pay taxes, which he could do in kind. The village chief needed service more than he needed money."

He paused and took a quick sip from his glass, then went on with his story as everyone leaned towards him.

"My father was a practising Muslim and sought to have me grow up a perfect man. He brought me up under the rigid prescripts of the Holy Book of Allah, the Koran, portions of which I learnt to recite as a little boy in the village school, and passages of which I wore in the form of charms and amulets, for protection and luck. For the first few years of childhood, life appeared to promise me nothing short of greatness. My family was in tune with Allah who was gentle with us. Had things been allowed to take their course, I might have grown up to be a master, not a servant. I might have become a man of considerable affluence and influence, and who knows? Perhaps I would be in a position today to tell Musa, Hassan and their factions to stop destroying and start building. But things hardly go the way one would like to have them go. We fart, but instead of the wind blowing the stench away from us, it blows it right into the very nostrils that we seek to protect. The greatness promised by my childhood was never to be. What can we do? Nothing! Absolutely nothing."

"Nothing," Chopngomna, Margarita and the others echoed, to show that they totally agreed with Dieudonné's view of the world. Their experiences had taught each and everyone of them that one didn't always have what one wanted out of the world, and that more often than not, there was really little one could do to influence the stubborn humiliations of life.

Dieudonné knew all about drinking – he certainly knew what he needed to keep going. So when he felt a little blocked, he stopped and fetched his snuffbox, poured some of the snuff into his palm whence he took it in bits and applied to his nostrils. Then he sneezed and sneezed, and felt decongested. Chopngomna and a diminutive little man three seats to his left asked him for some, which they equally took in to clear their heads, and to purge their nerves of any signs of tiredness. After bouts of sneezing, Dieudonné resumed his story. Precious came around to listen to him whenever she was not serving, dividing her attention between Dieudonné and Dieumerci whom she was sure was talking to her with his eyes. On her lovely t-shirt, struggling with her breasts for prominence, were the bold-lettered inscription: 'Guaranteed To Be Disappointed', as if in response to what was written on the back of the same t-shirt: 'Essayon Voir'.

"Then came the time when the quiet of the village was disrupted. It was not of our making, but the result of forces from beyond. Long before World War II my father was conscripted into Muzunguland's colonial army and sent to defend Muzungulander interests in Muzungu-Avenir. My father took me along with the hope of continuing with his mission to build a perfect man of me in the image of Allah.

"Muzungu-Avenir was a Muslim country like the part of Warzone we came from, and my father believed it wouldn't be too difficult to find someone who could offer me, 'un véritable enfant de la brousse' – a real bush child in those days, the relevant education, Insha'Allah, while he fought for the honour of Muzunguland.

"After seven years and above, all I succeeded to become in Muzungu-Avenir was a shoe mender. I worked for an Arab who had learnt the trade in City-of-A-Thousand-Camels," Dieudonné cast his mind back to his first day at the shoe mender's workshop: peng, peng, peng … the cobbler had hammered away at the sole of shoes, making him wince with pain, doubting if he would cope, which eventually he did, imbibing the motto: 'no pain, no gain.' It was that same day – how can he forget that part of the city he lived where a strong local black beer distilled from grain and dates was frowned upon vigorously! – when he had his first taste of Hamoud, a popular lemonade that had become an icon of local resistance to imported pleasures. The cobbler had offered him this drink, like some sort of bait for him to join the honourable profession of shoe mending. And it must have worked, since he stayed. Or was it for lack of options?

"But shoe mending wasn't a good business because the resident Muzungulanders scarcely needed their shoes repaired, and even when the need arose as was the case in the army from time to time, they preferred to make a shipload of soldiers' boots which they sent to Muzunguland for faster and better, even if more expensive, repairs. On their part, the struggling natives had more important matters of daily bread, dates, butter and sugar for mint tea to worry about than the purchase of luxury shoes. Advertisements such as: 'tant que les hommes auront les pieds, pas un pas sans Bata', simply did not mean much. Many ordinary Arabs wore what we the shoe menders wore ourselves, a type of tough leather slippers that defied wear and tear," Dieudonné giggled. "Similar to the rubber slippers you Mimbolanders have nicknamed: 'the tailless cow depends on Allah to keep the flies off its bum'. Among my native Warzoners where the white man was transported around on sedan chairs by hefty, bare-foot, young black beasts of burden, the rumour was that shoes were so hurtful that whites rarely walked when they had them on."

"When my father and I came back home after a very long absence, our little village near Warzone City had changed remarkably," Dieudonné went on, wetting his lips with the tip of his tongue. He was enjoying his own story. He stole a look at Dieumerci. The young man's Guinness was untouched. "Drink your drink, my boy," he urged. "My story isn't going to run away. We are in a social gathering, are we not?"

"I know," said Dieumerci, picking up his drinking glass. "I'm sorry, but your story is more drink than a drink," he added, looking a bit embarrassed. "Do you need some more drinks?" he asked Dieudonné, thinking, what a silly question to ask a fish.

"No, young man," replied Chopngomna, the great supplier with a generous wallet. "Keep your coins in your pocket," he said with a laugh. "I'll give Munding Swine Quarter all the Beaufort bien glacée he wants, do you understand?" He pulled his left ear to indicate the channel he wanted his message to take. At the same time, he pulled out a wad of crumpled banknotes from the inner pocket of his kaftan and waved it towards Dieumerci. "This round of drinks, and the next and the next and the next for everyone here present – all on me," Chopngomna offered with a mocking laugh, like the real 'moni man' that he was, to the sound of great applause.

The others laughed and made some silly remarks about students, how miserable and dependent they were, yet ever so keen to show off the nothing they had. Dieumerci felt insulted, but he was in no mood to compromise his chances of hearing Dieudonné's thrilling life story. He adopted the spirit of the place and smiled over every stupid comment. In another time and place, he most certainly would have challenged them to prove that they had earned the money they were now sending down the drain.

Dieudonné was supplied two more cold King Sizes by the generous giver. A middle-aged man of medium height, accompanied by two young women of average beauty, had come into the Grand Canari and joined the ranks. Dieudonné's slightly broken voice, which was midway between a child's and an adult's, and his mixture of Muzungulandish and Pidgin, fascinated the ears. All these, added to his narrative style and sense of humour, made Dieudonné the king of laughter. But that was when what he said called for laughter. Sometimes listeners couldn't hold back the tears of happiness and sadness that his story articulated in them.

Dieudonné thanked his friend profusely and continued his story.

"Yes, our village had changed an awful lot. Many of the old people we had left behind were dead and buried by the time we got back. My father, who missed them sorely, soon found out that he was about the most senior man around. But the village had ceased to be what it used to be. Almost every young man of fighting age had been swept off by the Muzungulander tides of war to fight their lives away in remote parts of Asia and Europe. Had my father not lost a leg defending Muzunguland's right to rule Muzungu-Avenir, he would have been sent to fight elsewhere. But having been handicapped as a Muzungulander soldier, he was to remain one for the rest of his life. In principle, he was to be paid a pension; in reality it was never done. He had wasted away his life for Muzunguland, a master who was in no hurry to discover the meaning of gratitude. As for me, I was still not fully ripe to kill enemies of Muzunguland with a gun. Had I been of the right age, I'm certain they wouldn't have stopped for a while to think that my father was handicapped and might need my support," Dieudonné shook his head disapprovingly.

"When we returned home, we found among other things that my four junior sisters had grown into big women, all of them, but had no husbands to marry. Like my father and the other conscripts, they were all victims of war, as captured in a song I was later to be taught by the daughter of a master I served in Sawang. Perhaps you know the song. It goes like this:

> Where have all the flowers gone
> Long time passing
> Where have all the flowers gone
> Long time ago
> Gone to young girls everyone
> When will they ever learn?

The young girls in turn go to young men who become soldiers, who end up in graveyards that yield beautiful flowers to feed young girls with ambitions of romance."

The audience found the song very moving, and Margarita insisted that Dieudonné should continue singing until she had caught the words and tune, which she did eventually. Only then did Dieudonné continue with his story.

"The situation in Warzone was worse than that in the song as the Muzungulander lions of war seemed keen to make widows of women even before they had found a husband to marry. My mother was attaining middle age already, enfeebled by encroaching blindness and repeated struggles with the guinea worm. Her last words to me, 'Je ne vois pas bien mais je ne peux ne pas reconnaître ma chaire,' how can I forget them? Annoyed that many able-bodied young men had been taken to the war front, the village elders and women were planning to boycott cotton farming, in which they found a loss of personality and welfare. But I wasn't in the village long enough to know what happened. All I know is that today, Warzoners still produce cotton for which they receive very little in return from the Muzungulanders who need it, and that they still kill one another in the name of foreign interests. I stayed at home for three days, no more, no less.

"On the third day after our return, I called to see my father and told him that I was leaving home. 'I'm going away father,' I said in tears. 'Now that I've brought you back home, I'm going away,' I told him, with pain in my heart. But he didn't ask me where I was heading. My mother asked me neither, nor did my sisters. None asked me where I was going. They stayed mute as if their tongues had been stitched with cotton thread, the Muzungulander's love. So I left home, the village and my country, pulled out by a force I could neither describe nor resist. I couldn't even say where I was going. Like cotton fibre, I simply drifted in the direction of the wind, the only thing I was conscious of. Allah is Great, for sure."

Dieudonné stood up, excused himself, and went out to free his bladder. He was followed by some of the others, Dieumerci included.

Bonblanc Mukala Ni-Ni and his women snatched the opportunity and asked Precious to turn on the music. This time, it was Prince Eyango's 'Take Moni Leave Ma Head' that they wanted. Precious obliged. Bonblanc Mukala Ni-Ni and his women, sachets of 'whisky condom' in hand, danced and sang along:

> 'I give a smile
> You want a handshake
> When I give a handshake
> You want a hug
> But I give a hug
> You want a kiss
> But when I give a kiss …'

CHAPTER EIGHT

Dieudonné returned to the bar, his fingers and trousers soaked in urine. He wiped his fingers on the body of his sweating bottle, picked up his glass, and smiled as he refilled it. "Ma mop tak'am. Man yi own na man yi own," he gulped. Then he exclaimed: "Afta life na die!"

A little girl who had followed him in complaining that he had splashed urine on her tray of puff balls as she gave change to a customer was summarily dismissed by Chopngomna: "Take that and leave Dieudonné alone." He handed her MIM$100. The girl took the money and left the bar shouting: "Buy your puff balls, excellent quality! … Puff-puff, eh!"

The music was again turned off. When everyone had settled down, Dieudonné resumed his story.

"I left home determined to start afresh," he told his audience. "I felt wasted, nothing like a man. It was as if I could barely, barely crawl, not even dreaming yet of walking or running. The feeling of a wasted youth was profound in me. 'It's perhaps the toughest and darkest valley of my life, but even this will come to pass,' I consoled myself."

Dieudonné looked around. Everyone was giving him attention. He went on.

"Then I found myself in Mimboland, after a strange journey through strange places, with strange encounters that included a narrow escape from the fangs of an angry mountain spitting fire-melting rocks and sinking entire villages. How true the saying that nothing is impossible with Allah! If you are in tune with Allah the Almighty, if you plan and think with Him, nothing would be above you, for nobody can say no where Allah has said yes. I cracked through situations that would ordinarily have devoured anyone.

I slept with rotting corpses in killing fields abandoned in a hurry by departing Muzungulanders, went for days without water as I trekked through the desert, was chased by lions for long distances through the northern grasslands, almost eaten up by giant crocodiles as I struggled across a hungry river brown with mud, survived by sucking pebbles at one point, and grounded by malaria and swollen feet in the heart of the rainforest littered with tombstones that told the triumphs of mosquitoes over Muzungulanders who had ventured too far. Well enough to use my feet again, I resumed my journey of a thousand dangers. I passed through a village with hundreds of people, none of whom could see a thing, none of whom knew a thing beyond sitting by the roadside, their beggar's bowls outstretched. Talibe, they were called. In the morning they would line up the sides of the roads into the village hoping for food and money from strangers and passers-by. I had nothing for them but prayers in abundance, which I doubt they took kindly. When I crossed the frontiers, I had neither a *laissez-passer*, nor a *carte d'identité nationale*, nor tax tickets of any kind. Yet I went through like a magician. No problem that I faced was insurmountable. Almost blinded by the fluid of a strange fruit I had harvested in desperation to assuage my grumbling belly, I was lucky enough to stumble on a hunter who kindly took me to his village. There, he washed my eyes with special herbs and introduced me to his chief who offered me food and shelter, and who asked one of his retainers to teach me their language. I failed to learn much. Had I learnt beyond the greetings and the names of the days of the week, they might probably have asked me to stay and belong. So I left, taking with me their prayers for Ataa-Naa-Nyongmo, their 'Father-Mother-God', to bless my way. Today I mostly remember that village as the land where each day of the week had a female and a male name, and girls and boys were named after the day they were born. For the girls, there was Adzo for Monday, Abena for Tuesday, Aku for Wednesday, Yawo for Thursday, Afi for Friday,

Ama for Saturday and Esi for Sunday. For the boys, it was Kojo, Kwabena, Kweku, Yao, Kofi, Kwame, and Kwesi. At one point I found myself at a region where I encountered Tougalish for the first time. Ugh! What a hell of problems I had there! I came to the town of Lola, where mass recruitment of plantation labourers for the Mimboland Development Corporation was in process. From the experiences of peasants back home, I preferred death in any form than to work in a plantation. To be physically flogged by such a weakling as a Muzungulander is too much for some of us." Dieudonné heaved a sigh and shook his head dejectedly. Then he went on with the story, his Mimbolander listeners ever more attentive.

"Do you know that a farmer can flourish in such strange crops as cotton, cocoa and coffee, yet die of famine? If you don't, let me tell you that these crops have no immediate value as food. You can't eat cotton, can you?" Everyone shook their head in denial; these crops were not the type to stop starvation. They are meant to inflame with hunger.

"Another disadvantage," Dieudonné continued, "is that with these crops, one toils so much for so little in return. Not only were the farmers in Warzone lowly paid for the cotton they made possible, like cows during drought, they ate only to enable them to be milked afresh. The little they got in return for the cotton they produced was again swept away by taxes, medicines and school fees for children. So much so that villagers who spent their whole time farming cotton ended up with neither money nor food, which they failed to cultivate because of lack of land, or because the district officer would not let them. In some cases, forced to choose between terror by the Muzungulander and enslavement by Arabs further north, a good number of my people, young women in particular, went the Arab way." Bitterness oozed from his words.

"It was an oppressive regime," he said, his voice choking with emotion. "In fact, so oppressive was it that some farmers decided to react despite the dangers. As my grandmother used to say, the child who carries his sorcery into adulthood has chosen a bed of nails. The colonial district officer was that child, and he had carried his sorcery beyond the point where people would normally look before they leaped. So some peasants devised a technique of silent protest. They would cultivate the cotton quite alright, forced to as they were, but they would come back at night when the oppressive district officer, his gendarmes and watchdogs had retired to their homes, to spray the young plants with a deadly powder which they imported from neighbouring Greenbook Republic. In the case of the mature cotton plants, I knew some of the peasants who would secretly lead the cattle of nomadic herdsmen into the plantations to eat up the leaves and the buds. In both instances, the peasants sought to save face, not to appear to accept to be trampled upon and humiliated at will by their taxing overlords. Their efforts were feeble and their successes few at the end of the day, but their spiritual satisfaction was enormous, and gave them reason to hope for better years, if not for themselves, for their children at least."

Dieumerci wrote at length in his notebook. He had read of everyday resistance. Now, thanks to Dieudonné, he knew that it had served the peasants of Warzone. The rest were all things academics had investigated and written about but this touch of personal experience was missing in most books and scholarly publications.

After finishing his Guinness and accepting another, Dieumerci again felt like going out to humour his screaming bladder. But he also did not want to miss a thing, so he suppressed the urge for a little longer and stayed on to listen, as Dieudonné recollected his past.

"In the town of Lola, which I mentioned earlier, the agents in search of unskilled plantation labour tried to recruit me. But when they realised that I was a slow learner and that all I could speak was Muzungulandish, which they neither understood nor cared much about, they nicknamed me 'useless frog' and allowed me to go my way. Their decision to set me free wasn't immediate though. It came only after a long period of tormenting and tossing me up and down the town, from one administrative department to another besides futile attempts to convince me that I was not from Warzone as I claimed to be. They had even tried to teach me their language – Tougalish – but I fared very poorly in it, much to their fury, as somehow, they were of the belief that anyone worth his place in their world needed to prove himself in Tougalish. Perhaps in the end they had thought that they would be better off without me in their banana, palm oil, rubber, cocoa and coffee plantations that were situated in the coastal region of West Mimboland.

"Allah alone knows why they chose to let me go my way. Why had they called me 'useless frog'? I still recall how confused I was by their decision, and how I wondered much about it, trying to guess just what had forced them to turn me down. I tried to find out what they thought of Muzunguland and Muzungulandish. Perhaps from some unpleasant past experiences, they had come to consider Muzungulandish as the language of troublemakers, crooks, spies, dissemblers, noisemakers and weaklings – something parents used to frighten their children into compliance. Apart from these speculations, I have never really known why those agents preferred to let me go my way when I was aware that they would readily have bribed a local chief to have more of his energetic young men."

Dieudonné emptied his glass, excused himself once more and went out to make water behind the bar. Dieumerci also seized the opportunity to attend to his ranting bladder. While both were still behind the bar, Chopngomna and the other men joined them. Urination was generally contagious and thought to come about more by induction. When one person in a group started it, others followed suit as if everyone had been waiting for someone to take the lead. When the men regained their seats, Margarita and the other women took their turns. Thousands of thick dark flies returned to enjoy the windfall that had unsettled them with splashes of urine, torn as they were between the meat roaster nearby and the appeal of fresh intoxicated urine at the open air urinary where bees were foraging for essential ingredients.

Wiping his hands this time on his shirt, Dieudonné offered to wait for the women to return before resuming his story. Meanwhile he asked Precious to uncap another of his King Sizes, which he began to sip with an imitation of kingly dignity.

CHAPTER NINE

The village was exhausted from the waiting. The sun spread its rays brightly as if in defiance of the event. Finally the huge lorry with its load of men clad in green clothes appeared. They did their business promptly without talking to anyone. First the casket was offloaded. All the villagers gathered gasped in shock. His only leg was out… The eldest villager came forward on crutches, to inspect what had become of the eldest living son of the soil. He opened the casket, what he saw disgusted him beyond measure. The body lay crumpled, like a foetus, hands drawn to the back, like a captured slave. He looked at the head of the men in green clothes, spat on the ground and ordered the young men to remove the body from the undersized casket. Jeering, the crowd took the body away, leaving the mouths of the men in green clothes agape.

"Stunted in life by their wars and injustices, my father was to be stunted in death by their mockery of a coffin. I am glad the village rejected the thing," Dieudonné interjected with satisfied defiance, waking up to his expectant audience. He was thinking of his late father.

"I learnt of my father's death through an accidental meeting at Sawang with a youth from my home village," Dieudonné told them. "This young man named Mbaisso was looking for a disappearing Muzungulander who had promised to sponsor his education in Muzunguland after convincing him to give up on the wife his father was seeking for him and on having anything to do with women. So he had come asking among the Muzungulander residents in the coastal city of Sawang, as the address indicated, but most he enquired from laughed and called him naive. I was employed as gardener to one of the Muzungulander colonial officers at the time

– my first real job in Mimboland as you may rightly guess – and that is how I met Mbaisso. He was a very nice and understanding young man with a voice that radiated sunshine who had come to accept through bitter disappointments that life reserves its true meaning for the daring and the trusting. So when he was told that there was no Muzungulander in the locality by that name and address, Mbaisso threw the whole affair behind him and joined me. We worked together for five months. He had to earn enough money to sponsor his trip back home. He insisted he wanted to be around on Uhuru Day to partake of the truth of growing rumours announcing 'deep, deep wells of oil' buried in the belly of the soil of Warzone that should deliver 'big, big money' to those present when the pregnancy was due. I empathised with the young man's right to dream, suppressing a part of me that felt like saying: 'I hope you don't have to wait, and wait, and wait for your oil baby, and that if it does come, you can sing and dance and dream like parents do when their child is born.' As if to be there to prove him wrong in future, I invited him to the popular Ever-Ready-Photo-Studio nearby where we were photographed together, two copies of which photo I insisted on him taking back with him – one for my family, and the other for his future remembrance." Hands akimbo and face straight up, Dieudonné demonstrated how he had posed for the photograph, against a dream background of the modern conveniences that lured all and sundry in those days.

"During the months we spent together, I learnt from Mbaisso all that there was to know about Warzone. It was he who told me of my father's death in a battlefield, fighting for the Muzungulander. At first I found Mbaisso's story hard to swallow. 'My father was an invalid when I left home, wasn't he?' I reminded the young man. 'He had lost a leg fighting for Muzunguland in Muzungu-Avenir, hadn't he?' Mbaisso nodded. 'Then how could he have gone fighting again? Certainly not my father!' I protested, unable to hold back my tears. But Mbaisso knew what he was telling me to be true. He revealed how the Muzungulander had invited my father back to the battlefront when the going was tough for Muzunguland. Though my father complained, no one paid attention to him. So he died fighting. Fighting for the Muzungulander. His dying words: 'Vive le Muzunguland.'" Dieudonné tried to prevent himself from crying, but everyone could see that his eyes were clouded with tears. And nobody would blame him for crying. "And as if they hadn't insulted my father enough, the Muzungulander military authorities sent an undersized coffin for his burial," he added. It was clear, his bitterness. "Was this poverty an evidence of the wastefulness of war? Or was it contempt for those who sacrificed even their lives to give Muzunguland a felt presence in colonial Warzone and beyond?"

Dieudonné knew the answer to his own question. He had heard from others accounts of how the Muzungulanders had treated their African ex-combatants with incredible shabbiness despite their sacrifices in preserving Muzunguland from destruction. How could they have rounded up and repatriated in a hurry and in shame, with little to show for years wasted away in war, Africans who had done them proud as beasts of burden? How could they have descended so low as to execute and bury in mass graves in the heart of night, ex-combatants who had dared to claim the same rights and entitlements as their Muzungulander counterparts? If black soldiers had outperformed their white counterparts in shedding blood 'pour la patrie', why were they being made to believe that the Muzungulander army had two laws, one for whites and the other for blacks? And how could a mighty power like Muzunguland stoop so low as to extort from homeless soldiers maimed and raped of dignity by dirty wars even the mere pittance paid them, using as excuse the fallacy that blackness and comfort were never meant to be good bedfellows? Did they really think that it was by exploiting thousands of helpless and mostly dismembered black ex-combatants that Muzunguland was to undo the destruction of war?

"Mbaisso also told me that the Muzungulander colonial office would not pay my father's war allowances and pension to anyone else but me. 'Why me?' I asked, but Mbaisso couldn't say more. If that was their policy, which made absolutely no sense to me, then they could keep the money to themselves. I refused to go back home because I didn't decide to come to Mimboland. 'Destiny brought me here, and destiny will have to take me back home. But for now, I'll rush nothing. Que sera sera,' I told Mbaisso. When he was going back home, I asked him to greet everyone and to tell my mother and sisters to be patient with me. 'Tell them that I shall come home in the same way that I left, Insha'Allah. There is a plan for every one of us, home and away. Whatever will be will be.'"

At this point Dieudonné started murmuring Remmy Ongala's 'No Money, No Life'. The song, whose lyrics he had mastered with time, was his favourite whenever he was down with homesickness. Heavy with sadness, Dieudonné swayed his head as he sang:

'Heh young brother, come close to me
I need you, come close to me brother
I want you to take my greetings back home
Tell my grandmother that I am still sweating in town
I want you to take my greetings back home to the village
Tell my grandfather that I am still sweating in town
Life in town needs more money
If you don't have money you will suffer
If you don't have money you will never sleep
If no money you can never eat
You won't even wash your clothes
Everybody needs money
Everybody needs more money
Life without money is like punishment
Life without money no respect'

"So Mbaisso left me and went back. I've heard nothing from him since. It is difficult to keep in touch when people are so far away, particularly when, like me, one has neither a permanent address nor a job that's sufficiently rewarding to motivate others to write requesting assistance. The message and photo I sent through Mbaisso happened to be my first and last to Warzone from Mimboland. Like all of you, my knowledge of the situation at home is second-hand. But I know that it is my place to do more than consume stale news. You are foreigners to my homeland. I'm not. What can I do? What do I have? When you talk of Dieudonné, this is all there is to me," he indicated his person. "I have nothing else in the world, nothing. I can't even fart the way a real man would. I am a nothing man. I am l'homme falsifié par la vérité", he repeated. "Sometimes I'm so bitter that I feel like telling everyone: 'Si tu voir un Muzungulandais avec un serpent tue d'abord le Muzungulandais avant de tuer le serpent.' But I know that wouldn't be fair, as there surely must be thousands of good Muzungulanders, even if few have come my way. It can't all be 'kif kif'."

"Someone once said: 'The less intelligent the Muzungulander, the more he takes the Mimbolander for a fool'." Dieumerci agreed.

"However despicable the Muzungulanders we meet, we must remember, as my mother used to say, that if we close our eyes in order not to see evil, we just might miss the truth when it passes," Dieudonné remained measured, despite his bitterness.

A pause imposed itself on the scene. Chopngomna warned: "Watch out for little girls selling chewables!" and was greeted by hilarious laughter. "I'm out of coins," he added, and joined the rest.

"I have been in Mimboland for over forty years," resumed Dieudonné when everyone was back and had taken their seats. "But I have never set foot in Warzone since I left decades ago." His voice shook slightly with guilt. "I know that much has changed back home. You know for instance about the fighting that is raging there. My father died shortly after I left. That I know very well." Dieudonné stared at the beer in his glass and added, "That's life," more to himself than to his audience. "May his soul be preserved, Dieu est grand," said he, supporting his head with his left hand.

Everyone sympathised with Dieudonné at this point. They understood how painful it was not to be present to bury one's father. Dieumerci thought of the enigma of war. Why was it that the people who wanted wars the most were the least likely to be found at the warfront defending what they had ignited? Why was it that ordinary soldiers, innocent civilians and harmless communities were ravaged the most by war when they contributed the least to making a case for it? Top politicians and powerful people were seldom the losers, always able to escape into safety when everyone else was dying, and their private interests sure to triumph over the impoverishments of war – a classic case of wearing a public helmet to run a private race.

"I have spent all these years working for the Muzungulander. My father fought his wars for him. I have weeded his garden, tended his plants, cooked for him and his pets, and kept his dresses neat and clean, so that he should stay white and tall. My family seemed to have been created to cater for the Muzungulander in war and in peace, in sickness and in health. War kills violently, which is why my father died abruptly. But because peace kills slowly, I'm fading away unattended. My wounds are internal, bleeding despair and unhappiness. My father's wounds were external, which is why we all shared his grief and bore his physical burdens with him." He paused, then added: "So I have worked for Muzungulanders ever since I came to Mimboland, preserving their magic and mystic, just like my father did, and looking up to them prayerfully, hoping for luck, if and when it pleases them to smile on me."

He was in no hurry to enter this phase of his fascinating story without inducement, knowing that none of those sitting with him had shared the same privilege of working for Muzungulanders in intimate circles.

"If you want to hear the juiciest part of my life story yet, make it worth my while. If the Muzungulander has taught me anything all these years of serving and servicing him, it is simple: Nothing goes for nothing; nothing is impossible; nothing in, nothing out; you can't reap where you haven't sown; everyone for himself and Allah for us all; winner takes all; money is power, information is money; knowledge is the name of the game; once houseboy, always a boy, toujours jeune." He smiled mischievously, and the beer flowed, including one for the insistent and curious Dieumerci, from Chopngomna, the man with the bleeding wallet, who was known to have inscribed above his desk at the office for every visitor to see, the words: 'There is much happiness in giving than in receiving.' In that saying Chopngomna had identified himself with a proud tradition of the civil service, where a goat is meant to eat where it is tethered, and where it is normal and indeed to be celebrated, for someone 'wrongly' accused of illicit self-enrichment to put the records straight by declaring: "Ces sont les gratitudes et les servitudes de la fonction publique".

CHAPTER TEN

Servants are servants, masters masters. Dieudonné had never disputed that. He had always known his place, expecting those he served to master theirs. But few were the masters who had lived up to his expectations, or treated him with the dignity he needed to excel in service. For how can one harvest without planting? Suck without filling? Expect service without rendering service? Receive without giving? Not know that 'le pied droit a besoin du pied gauche pour marcher'? In short, how can a master be master without the servant -- the servant embedded in him as master, most especially?

"The general practice has been simple and straightforward," Dieudonné began to tell them the story of his experiences as an employee of the Muzungulander over the years. Everyone was interested to hear of the Muzungulander, stories about whom were always exciting, even if often grossly exaggerated.

"The first Muzungulander came my way by luck. I had been arrested by the Mimboland police for being an illegal alien and had been threatened with deportation when a white friend of the policeman in charge happened to call by. Upon seeing me, he immediately thought I would be much use doing his garden than being bundled back to Warzone. So he struck a deal with his friend, who turned a blind eye on my irregular status, and I was allowed to stay." He paused and took a look round, as if to ensure that everyone was listening. "Ma combi for musica like Douleur and Petit-Pays dem di sing 'travailleur immigré' and 'sans papiers' for Muzunguland today like say na new ting. 'Illegal aliens' na palaver wey yi old pass ndependa for all kontri for dis Africa," he observed.

"Unfortunately, the man himself, Monsieur Barbiers, was deported to Muzunguland for some crime I never quite understood.

But before leaving, he did what was to become a pattern. He passed me on to his brother, a fellow Muzungulander." Dieudonné shook his head in self-pity, although the Toubaabys would probably say self-pity was the only form of pity worth wasting on him.

"This particular one had a wife, a staunch Catholic, who would only hire me if I changed my pagan name to something more Christian. I still remember that conversation most vividly. 'Boy, what is your name?' her ladyship had asked, standing akimbo. 'My name is Allah-Go'onga,' I had told her, half timid. 'What sort of name is that?' she had retorted disapprovingly, and even before I had whispered: 'This is what my parents called me when I was born, and it means God Almighty', she had protested: 'I can't hire you with a name like that!' Desperate for a job, I asked myself: 'What's in a name?' So her ladyship took me to her parish priest who sprinkled a bowl of water on me and said: 'From now you become Dieudonné.' And that was how Dieudonné took over Allah-Go'onga, and has over the years imposed himself with an arbitrariness that shatters whatever sense of self that my inner self has been trying to cultivate. Baptised Dieudonné, I thanked the priest for his generosity and her ladyship for her benevolence. I served her faithfully for two years until the priest caught me eating 'meat' one Good Friday. 'Dieudonné, you are eating meat on Good Friday!' the priest screamed his disappointment. 'No, Father, it isn't meat, it is fish,' I insisted. 'And what is worse, you are lying to a man of God on Good Friday,' his fury grew. And when still I insisted it was fish not meat, he asked me to explain why I was claiming that it was fish when he was seeing meat. So I told him: 'Father, when you saw me, my name was Allah-Go'onga. Upon her ladyship's insistence, you took a bowl of water and sprinkled it on me and pronounced me Dieudonné. Similarly, I took meat, sprinkled some water on it, and pronounced the meat fish. If it worked for you as a priest, it should work for your disciples.' The priest left tongue-tied. At the end of that month, her ladyship paid me, and with the words 'God gives and God takes', she passed me on to a Muzungulander less fussy about who ate what on Good Friday." Dieudonné paused to drink his beer as his audience roared with laughter at what to him was clearly no laughing matter.

He continued his story. "I learnt my lesson from that experience, and have kept my tongue in check ever since. And as long as I have known my place, things have worked out somehow with my Muzungulander masters. And tradition has been kept, as I mentioned earlier. When one Muzungulander employed me and happened to come to the end of his stay in this country, he would introduce me to his brothers before leaving for good. The one who was interested received recommendations from the outgoing master with whom he also discussed the terms. And so they passed me from hand to hand like little puppies playing with a meatless bone. Never did any of them ask me how much wage I would like to be offered. The outgoing employer always supplied the new master with all the bits of information he needed in order to know how to handle their newly acquired servant. 'Dieudonné est ceci, Dieudonné est cela. Il aime ceci, il n'aime pas cela'. In this way my new master always had the advantage over me. He knew all about me, while I knew nothing about him, apart from his name, which I seldom was given the privilege to call. 'Monsieur' or 'Madame' suffices, and is recommended as healthy for the houseboy that I am. Often I use 'patron'. I know that a servant who calls his master by name is not a good servant and is likely to be given a bad testimonial. And who wants a bad testimonial in a job where the master's word is law?"

Everyone nodded.

"In the light of the set up, which I've just talked about, you realise that it was clearly up to my new master either to lay claim to generosity by adding a few centimes to my wages, or to stick to the rate pre-established by his predecessor. I had little say in the matter but to accept their decisions. Even where the new master was kind enough to increase my wages, I must be honest with you that the little they added was seldom enough to pay for an extra litre of palm oil. On the contrary, my workload was sure to increase as a result of the mythical *increment de salaire*, as they loved to term their gesture." Dieudonné laughed sardonically, belched and hit his chest as if to say, 'despite all the hardship, I've survived to tell you my life story'.

He looked around him. Everyone was listening. 'My story must be very interesting,' he thought, quite encouraged. He put down his drinking glass and fetched his snuffbox from his trouser pocket. There were candidates as usual willing to share his snuff with him. After the sneezing that followed had died down, Dieudonné returned to his story.

"I've worked in Sawang, Sambang, Loumah and here in the capital city," he told them. "For the first twenty years of my stay in Mimboland, I worked in Sawang and Sambang alone. It was during that time that I learnt the most about South Mimboland, and that I became accepted by Mimbolanders as one of them. Then I started feeling at home away from home. Today, unless I tell someone that I'm from Warzone, he can't suspect that I'm not a Mimbolander. It was also during those first twenty years that I learnt to express myself in Pidgin, a language that I found to be particularly suiting to me and the other men that worked for the Muzungulander. We came to adore Pidgin because it was the language in which we could discuss our secrets, insult our masters, and plot coups without the Muzungulander overhearing and thwarting our plans.

"I had many friends among West Mimbolanders, one of whom, Masa Chief Cook Godwill Kakakaka – nicknamed 'Ashia-no-di-helep-but-yi-di-cool-heart' because of the frequency with which he stammered the expression, I shall never forget. He was the head cook to the Muzungulander director of a timber company – Raser les Tropiques – in Sawang, and we used to drink at the

Old Mariner, a bar situated not too far away from what was the Sawang seaport in those days. I loved the way he walked and would dance stylishly as if he had two left legs, or like someone whom jiggers had taught a lesson in childhood. The day we became friends was when, sitting by me at the Old Mariner, he pointed across and said: 'Ma combi, let me tell you a thing about drinking. You see those two people sitting over there? When you begin to see them double, know it is time for you to go home.' I looked and did not dare tell him I didn't see anyone sitting where he pointed. 'My name na Chief Cook Godwill Kakakaka,' he offered his hand. 'I be Dieudonné,' I replied. 'Do you sometimes wish you were a drunkerman?' he asked. 'Like life go be easy time no dey,' he added, not waiting for an answer. We became friends. Chief Cook Godwill Kakakaka taught me how to dance Bottle Dance – 'Abuimgah Nsteng', his favourite music from his very own home area. And he was particularly fond of songs such as 'Nedorrh' – Happiness, 'Nezoh' - Marriage, 'A kone' – Love, and 'Akwatee' – Help. When he had had enough to drink, he would insist on dancing 'fox throw' and 'kiss your partner' with me, singing along and adding such sayings as: 'a hungry man is an angry lion'; 'a man is a man because of a man'; 'a woman is an airport, a man an aeroplane'; 'woman kills man, money kills woman – man for woman, woman for money'; 'the magic of marriage: those out are dying to get in, those in desperate to get out'; 'do not hurry in life or your shadow will overtake you'; 'Fowl wey yi no di hear shiiii go hear mbam'; and 'be unlimited.'

"Unfortunately, he died in a car accident, on his way home to the village to return his 'unbroughtup' wife to her parents and ask for his money back, following his narrow escape from an attempt by her to savage his penis with a blunt kitchen knife. 'I marry po-po-po-popo baaaaluck!' he used to curse himself. His wife had shamed him repeatedly, to the extent even of boasting the day she was caught in a compromising situation with another man: 'He was so big he went to places my husband has never been.' And as if to hurt her husband's feelings even more, she had dramatised to a group of sympathetic women assembled to celebrate her blissful experience: 'Oliba show me wonder. Oliba make me hear fine. Oliba sweet pass pepper. Oliba sabi do'am pass all man. When Oliba dey for ma corner, na dasso one ting I di tell'am – masa hold me fine maka hear fine.' And he loved to say of his wife, when his stammering allowed him, that is: 'You fool me today you no go fool'am tomorrow. Even blind man want for sleep he go cover he eye. Any man like truth, even lie man like truth. Truth too di sweet for lie man.' I knew the wife very well, and was often terrified by the sort of treatment she gave him. Tall, huge and frightfully authoritative, she used to beat the poor chap up mercilessly, screaming: 'Today na today. You go see pepper with you eye.' And then would throw herself on the floor and pretend she was crying because her husband had beaten the hell out of her: 'Helep, helep, helep! Ma Masa don kill me. Make wena come helep before yi finish'am.' At first I didn't know that was the trick she played, and so together with other friends and colleagues of Masa Chief Cook Godwill Kakakaka, I used to curse him for maltreating his wife. If he could manage it, he would say: 'Let me stammer you the truth, my friends.' He would stammer, swear and on top of his little voice would plead that things were much more complicated than we thought. He had told me how he came to be married to his wife, how he had sent home a photo of himself with his left foot placed on a transistor radio wearing a hat, sunglasses, khaki shirt and shorts, thick socks, and leather sandals all borrowed, and how this particular woman had beaten every other village girl to it, and her father, for some strange reason, had asked for a bride price which even a man in borrowed gear could afford. She had hated him when she discovered that he was much barer than the photo had suggested. We often used to laugh at his voice which was as flat as an opened bottle of King Size left unattended." Dieudonné shook his head before adding, "Die no di ring bell. If yi ring bell sep, you deaf, you no go hear."

Everyone nodded, some saying, "na true."

"I miss him," Dieudonné continued. "I also miss the unforgettable stories he used to share with us, like this one. Apparently, in West Mimboland more than anywhere else, funerals have become an industry offering the living an opportunity to keep hope alive through food, drink and more.

"A West Mimbolander who had made a lot of money working in the city died and was brought for burial in his home village. Four young men took a look at his coffin and thought it would be a waste to use it only once. It could fetch them a lot of cash back in the city. So at night, after the big man had been laid to rest and the village had gone to bed, they came back, dug him up and stole the coffin, his jewellery, suit, shoes, genitals and head. On their way to the city to make money, they came to a checkpoint. One of the young men thought fast and asked the others to place the coffin on his head. At the checkpoint, a policeman asked: 'Where are you going with a coffin in the dead of the night?' The young man, like a tortoise who for want of relatives carries its own coffin wherever it goes, complained angrily: 'I be say dis village too hot, dat when I die make dem bury me for cold place, but dem no hear! I di go for cold place …' The policemen did not wait for him to finish. They fled!"

Dieudonné could sense from the atmosphere that this was not exactly the story his audience wanted and he was soon proved right when Margarita asked him to revert to his own story and experiences as a servant of the Muzungulander. He would keep the story of his good friend Masa Chief Cook Godwill Kakakaka for another occasion, another place and, most certainly, another audience.

"As far as wages are concerned," Dieudonné conceded, stopping to clear his throat, "what my former white masters paid me wasn't much, and what the Toubaabys pay me today isn't much either. But I thank Allah for getting by."

Turning to Dieumerci, Dieudonné said, "Dieumerci, I believe you saw how full of cracks and holes my house is? Yet I accept things the way they come. Do you know how much I pay for that poor, empty, good-for-nothing, rat-infested room every month?"

Dieumerci shook his head.

"MIM$6,000!" shouted Dieudonné. "No lights, no water, no window, no door, no floor, nothing. I have neither a good bed nor a chair. Where even do I get the food to eat? And when I sit in my house, passers-by and little children playing in the yard can see me through numerous openings in the walls. At night, it's as cold as if I were sleeping outdoors in the biting desert nights of Warzone. Until Tsanga disappeared, the nights were not so cold. Another nuisance is the rats and cockroaches, which hold their daily meetings in my room without permission. Perhaps they don't think they need permission, given how porous my walls are. I don't mind. Nor do I blame them. All is in the hands of Allah whom I praise daily. Allah has a plan for everyone. If he's planned that I should be eaten up by rats and cockroaches, so be it."

He suppressed a dubious laugh, for he was neither light-hearted nor joking about what he said. His style might be humorous, but he was telling the story of his life. How could he blame others for laughing at what to them was just a story?

"My experiences with my white employers are many and diverse", Dieudonné continued. "Whatever the experience, I believe I have borne my fate the way a man should. Sometimes I have received presents of old clothes and worn-out shoes, in addition to a good testimonial of service. Such moments when I'm called up by the master and told: 'Dieudonné, prend ça, je te laisse ces habits et ces chaussures qui ne me plaisent plus,' have always been pleasant and reassuring."

He paused and thought for a while, then added: "However, I can't say that those who give are good while those who fail to give are bad. What matters to me is the reason for giving or failing to give. There are times when I would rather starve than accept a gift of food from someone arrogant and repulsive."

Everyone agreed, for they each had examples of people who would give only to humiliate their less fortunate fellows. Such givers-of-convenience, as they were called, wouldn't hesitate to chant like weaverbirds, broadcasting their generosity the world over. They gave in order to be noticed and appreciated, not because they saw the need to help their fellow humans in solving the jigsaws of life.

"I'd like to satisfy Dieumerci's curiosity to know how I came to be working for Monsieur and Madame Toubaaby," Dieudonné told the group as if seeking their approval. "It's as I've told you already: that the Muzungulander lives in constant collaboration with his brother. He isn't like the black man who hates to see his brother make progress. The Muzungulander shares what he knows with his brother, even if others suffer more as a result.

"I first came to know the Toubaabys through two Jesuit priests who employed me last. They used to love their beer, wine and whisky, those two, and I enjoyed having the dregs. They would tell their Mimbolander visitors that back in Muzunguland, making beer was the business of certain kinds of men of God known as monks who, on the doorway to their home, had inscribed the words: 'In Heaven there is no beer, that is why we must drink it here'. Their favourite wine was always accompanied by a delicious rotten cheese the name of which sounded like a bleating goat – 'Camembert'. When not very much in the mood for serious drinking, they would settle for a cocktail, which was either a Bloody Mary or an Angel's Kiss. The older of the priests, a rather bullish but funny little man, was, in addition to his drink, so fond of chicken neck that at one wedding reception party he was so impatient with the Reverend Sisters who had been asked to serve themselves first and were quite undecided on what drumsticks to settle for. He stormed to the food table and ordered: 'Mes Soeurs, écartez vos cuisses et je tire mon cou'."

The men exploded in laughter. The women frowned. Dieudonné sipped his beer innocently as if he didn't know why. He continued:

"These priests were transferred to the far-northern region of Mimboland. I would have liked to accompany them, had they suggested it, but they didn't. 'What is it that I have which you don't want, or is it something I lack that you want?' I remembered asking them, perplexed. Then they told me that where they were going was full of young men who would equally be in need of employment. 'What is yours is yours, what isn't yours isn't yours,' I reassured myself, wounded though I was. Had I accompanied them to the north, I would most certainly have ended up at home. For once at the town of Pousserim, all I would have done was to cross the big river and find myself in Warzone City! But because my plans somehow outpaced destiny, they failed to materialise. I have been reduced to waiting for the day when my plans and destiny shall tread hand in hand on the same footpath. Then I shall know it is exodus." Dieudonné sounded as philosophical as always. Did philosophy make its roots from the heart of frustration? Dieumerci contemplated without interrupting Dieudonné.

"So when the priests would not take me along with them," continued Dieudonné, "they forged an alternative plan. They talked to the Toubaabys. The Toubaabys were interested, and a meeting was arranged at the library of the Muzunguland Cultural Centre. There, Madame Toubaaby met me and dictated her terms, which I was obliged to accept, bearing in mind my late father's words that survival comes before comfort. From Muzunguland Cultural Centre, Madame Toubaaby drove me directly to their residence at Quartier Beverly Hills, where I started work instantly, and where I've toiled for the past five years." He heaved a heavy sigh.

"To be fair to the priests, though, they did leave me with something valuable – a basket of jokes that I have shared with everyone who cares to listen. Every evening when I had served them and they had eaten, drank coffee and retired to relax over a bottle of spirits, the priests would sit me down to tell a joke or repeat an old one. Among their favourites were the following.

"Au siècle dernier, les militaires africains qui arrivaient pour la première fois à Muzunguland, au restaurant reçoivent les cures dents à la fin du repas et disent: 'ça doit être bon parce qu'il n'en donne pas beaucoup.' Ils tentaient de manger les cure dents à la forchette." (In the last Century, African soldiers coming to Muzunguland for the first time, when served toothpicks in restaurants at the end of their meal would say: 'This must be good since they serve very little of it'. They tried to eat the toothpicks with their forks!)

Just like Dieudonné, the audience found this joke racist and belittling of Africans who had sacrificed so much for Muzunguland that refused to see them as anything more than 'les grands enfants' to be boy-boyed at will. They were equally disgusted by Dieudonné's second joke: "Les militaires africains en Muzunguland arrivaient difficilement à distinguer leur droits de leur gauches. Alors on leur mettait de la paille dans une botte et du pain dans l'autre. Et pour marquer les pas on entonnait: 'Paille', 'Pain'." (African soldiers in Muzunguland could hardly distinguish their right from their left. So straw was fitted into one boot and bread in the other. To make them march, they were told: 'straw, bread').

So Dieudonné shared with them his favourite joke, someone who had fallen out with the church had told him. "It is about a missionary in a remote part of Mimboland who came face to face with a famished lion. Frightened, he started to pray: 'Lord heavenly father, inspire upon this lion the sentiments of a Christian. Ready to pounce, the lion, on its part, started to pray: 'Lord God, bless this meal that I am about to receive and give to everyone their own share of missionaries.'"

Even before Dieudonné had said the last word of the joke, everyone was falling down with laughter.

When the laughter had died down and he had recovered, he continued. "Like everyone else, I have my likes and dislikes, but I bear hardship, just to survive. I've worked here in Mimboland for over forty years but have saved nothing because I've earned nothing. I can boast of nothing, no material wealth, no job satisfaction, nothing. I am a nothing man. Sometimes it takes a year or more of toil to purchase a cheap cotton shirt like this one that I'm wearing. I thank God for okrika! And I wouldn't have a King Size now and again, were it not for friends like you. Dieu est grand." A wide smile spread across his face. "But I try not to mind. It is the order of things that I should toil to make others rich and comfortable while staying poor and miserable. My wife, and only companion, has vanished, leaving no trace. Poor as I may be, theft is too mean to contemplate. I would rather die a pauper than steal," he affirmed.

"Though I may have worked for the Muzungulander all my life," he went on, his listeners as keen as ever, "it doesn't mean that I prefer the Muzungulander to the Mimbolander. I can work for either, so long as I'm paid for the work I do. To me, a master is a master, white or black. I don't discriminate on the basis of the colour of the skin. As I said before, among white men, you have good ones and bad ones. So is the case among black men. I want money, and money is money. There is no white or black money. My only regret, however, has been the fact that the more I toil the less money comes my way. My surname is Payless. Yet at my age, I am confined to getting by at the margins."

He emptied his glass and belched. He didn't seem too tired from talking for so long. There was every sign that he could continue for the next hour or so, and not feel tired, as long as he had enough beer to keep the ball rolling. There was the King Size, and Dieudonné was a tireless speaker by nature. As long as his listeners were keen, he would go on telling them the story of his life, the only thing he had to offer in return for their generosity.

Someone suggested a musical interlude, Chopngomna bought the idea, and Dieudonné asked and obtained 'Beza Ba Dzo', his favourite tune by the legendary golden voice and queen mother of Bikutsi, Anne-Marie Nzie, in memory of his beloved Tsanga, whom he still prayed and hoped to catch up with and reconnect with for the best. He was ready to seek her forgiveness for his failings as a greedy and talkative alcoholic husband, if only he could set eyes on her again. He danced to the tune with his eyes closed so he could visualise his Tsanga, whom he imagined was dancing along with him, holding tight, and bringing meaning back into his shattered life.

CHAPTER ELEVEN

Dieudonné likened himself to a bridge which many a Muzungulander had crossed over the turbulent waters of life, but which few had acknowledged. Reluctantly, he had come to the conclusion that the word 'thanks' was nowhere to be found in the rich vocabulary of the Muzungulander. Even the white men of God had failed to convince him otherwise. He didn't know what to make of the services squeezed out of him over the decades. Was it proper to term them a labour of love, love of labour, labour of hope, hope of labour, a bit of everything, or something completely different?

"Ngundu work no go finish for dis ground," he concluded. "It is nice to be important, but it is more important to be nice," he added, philosophically. "How can you want to stay a master when you don't know what it feels like to be mastered?" he asked, rhetorically. He paused, deep in thought, then added in a slow deliberate tone: "Ceux qui mangent les oeufs ne savent pas combien la poule a suffert pour les pondre. Truth shared is truth tested."

"I can't name all the white men whom I've served since I came to Mimboland. In the course of serving them, I've gradually devised ways to limit my sufferings either by acting like the fool for which they take me, or by simply behaving as if my suffering were not there. But whenever I remarked that a particular master was making matters unduly difficult, I didn't escape by night or do anything silly. Rather, I went straight up to him and laid down my complaint. If he refused to limit his outrages and change his ways, I asked him to look for another servant because I had found it difficult to stay with him.

"When this happened, which wasn't often, some might pay me what they owed me in wages. Others would take advantage of the fact that I was leaving and refuse to pay. In either case, I went away all the same, convinced that it was the right thing to do, knowing that God is Almighty.

"There was no question of going to the police who, like me, were there to serve the same master. Any servant foolish enough to turn to the police for help against cruel masters lived to regret, if they survived the flogging that reporting a master brought. The first thing you learn in life is that the law is like a cobweb that entangles small flies but the big insects break through with impunity."

Everyone agreed.

"I've been employed by one Muzungulander or another," Dieudonné added, then paused.

For a while, he stared into his glass. "L'alcool tue la violence," he philosophised, before adding, "Now let's say something about our dear old friend – beer," he said, looking up at Chopngomna, who laughed and nodded.

"What about beer? C'est bon pour le moral, non?" Chopngomna asked, laughing. But not stopping to let Dieudonné explain himself, he added, "Go right ahead, Munding Swine Quarter. We are listening."

"Yes, we are listening," echoed Dieumerci, not allowing Dieudonné even the time to digress, his enthusiasm unchecked.

"Perhaps Dieudonné should have another drink," suggested Margarita. "Give him two more bottles," she told Precious, fetching her purse. "I'm paying for them," she insisted, and asked for another Amstel for herself as she threw her hair stylishly from side to side, her well-manicured fingers of gold-plated rings the centre of attention for the two women attending to Bonblanc Mukala Ni-Ni.

"Why did you think I should always be the one to pay?" inquired Chopngomna, rather light-heartedly. He recalled thinking she was joking the first day he dated her, when a stern-faced Margarita had made him understand her passions upfront in these words: 'Shopping is like climaxing. You don't want it to end when you are at it. But when you are through and you look at all the things you bought and the monies you've spent impulsively, you go like "hm! I don't want to do this again." And even sometimes you add, "What was the point?" but after a short while, you want to go back. You want that thrill again, that intoxicating and exhilarating sensation and you just don't care but you've got to have those clothes.'

"Who said you should pay?" she retorted.

"Because you women think that it's your birthright to receive from men, and that it's our duty to keep giving," he replied with an air of triumph.

"That's untrue!" Margarita exclaimed. "On the contrary it's you men who insist on giving despite our reluctance to accept. And once we've accepted your miserable gifts that cost virtually nothing, you go around singing how you took such and such out and gave her lots and lots to drink. You are braggarts! That's all you are – empty vessels that make the loudest noise," she concluded to the applause of the other women in the bar. "We don't want nobody to give us nothing . Open up the door and we'll get it ourselves. As women, we are what you shall never be: Well organised men."

The women exploded in congratulatory laughter. The men wanted to defend themselves, but they would wait for Dieudonné to finish his story. Like Chopngomna, most of them were too conceited to think of women as anything other than calculating, manipulative, ungrateful and tempting she-devils. They had all been schooled to underestimate women through simplistic and untested slogans such as: 'la logique des femmes prend le contre-pied de la logique dite normale ou positive. On ne sait jamais avec elles. Women, the graveyard of many a war hero. Women, fear dem more dan gamaline 20.'

"As I said a while ago," Dieudonné began, his glass full, "there is a strange thing that has gripped and numbed us all since the colonial days. Alcohol. Its presence is widespread. It has invaded and consumed us all, making ash of manhood and nonsense of women who dare smile its way. What a wonderful thing! I drink and fear alcohol at the same time. But I've learnt to cope with it over time. Today when I drink, I think of my job. This helps me to avoid taking too much, for I hate to stay away from work. But I've grown to depend so much on it that I wonder what I would do without my King Size."

Were Tsanga, his run-away wife present, she would have reminded Dieudonné of the number of times he had failed to go to work precisely because he had failed to master himself in front of alcohol the evening before. She would have told them that with him and alcohol, problems came in heaps, like bananas. She would have said that instead of serving as super glue to his social relationships, alcohol had numbed his instinct and appetite for great ambitions and made nonsense of his life. But with her away, the audience was unlikely to differentiate between his good intentions and what he actually did. Again, he couldn't resist thinking of his late friend and drinking partner of many years ago, Masa Chief Cook Godwill Kakakaka, who was always dramatic in the company of palm wine, the most affordable drink for the likes of him in those days: 'You drink you whisky you drunk, me I drink ma palm wine I drunk. Who drunk pass?' Masa Chief Cook Godwill Kakakaka would ask, and with a mocking laugh, would assert to great applause, 'Mimbo na mimbo. Bigman mimbo no savi drunk sep!' Then his call to modesty: 'The palm wine tapper who starts by falling off the tallest tree in the forest needs fear no fall.' But he had sensed that his audience wanted his story and not the story of others through him. And not wanting the tap of beer to dry up, he kept Masa Chief Cook Godwill Kakakaka's exciting and episodic life story to himself for the future and the right audience.

"Only a dead man can talk of complete abstinence from alcohol," Dieudonné postulated. "You see that even non-drinkers like my young friend Dieumerci," he smiled to the latter, "end up taking a bottle or two or three or ... Sometimes they become just as involved as we. Few are indifferent to the charms of the bottle, I would swear."

The others agreed.

"My principle is to drink, but not to drown my integrity," he added.

Others nodded.

"I would retort immediately if my employer says or does something that annoys me. I wouldn't wait to get drunk before confronting him. I don't need the courage of a drunkard for my anger to shine. But whenever I've dared to speak angrily to them, or when I've attempted to tell them the bitter truth about themselves, they've accused me of being drunk. I wonder if in Muzunguland, where they come from, one needs to be drunk to be truthful, or to express one's feelings. Are they all so cowardly, the Muzungulanders? I believe that to tell a lie is to die of truth we fear and loathe. The courage to criticise someone in his presence is, to me, preferable to the cowardice of doing so in his absence." Dieudonné was categorical about his convictions.

"I also wonder why despite their excessive riches, all the white men for whom I've worked have tended to be so thrifty. Quite unlike the rich black men we find around who go for all the expensive cars, the magnificent suits, the sparkling shoes, the big mansions and the most exorbitant wallet munchers. The black man displays his wealth on the tip of his nose. The Muzungulander wears his wealth like underpants. The one is surface rich, the other bottom rich. Perhaps their different attitudes to wealth explain why we are game for the Muzungulander to stalk. While the black man celebrates appearances, the Muzungulander banks on substance."

Dieudonné was interrupted with applause and murmurs: "What he says is true, quite true."

"The black man is like that, nice looking face, rotten heart."

"Yes, quite true indeed, we the black people think all that matters is to eat without thinking of tomorrow."

"The black man likes to think big, feel big, appear big, but achieve little."

"Big appetite, little tact."

"That's our tragedy," another one added, "Chop broke pot."

This went on for five minutes or so, while Dieudonné gulped more beer to keep him in the right mood to carry on. When the excitement died down, he resumed with what was rapidly becoming a sort of general social critique than merely a life story simply told.

"Talking about money," Dieudonné continued, "I can tell you that it has changed a lot since I came to Mimboland. Money is no longer the same thing that it used to be. There's been a great fall in its value, for one thing. When I started work decades ago, I was paid the equivalent of MIM$2 a month. Today, you may take it to be an incredibly tiny sum. But you are wrong to think in the same way in relation to the past, for money has value only within a particular point in time. My MIM$2 was big money in those days. With it, one could purchase a pair of trousers, a shirt and a pair of shoes, and also buy food, rent a room and enjoy oneself around town. First hand consumption, not hand-me-downs from Europe."

Dieudonné admired the look of bewilderment on the faces of his audience, but understood why they found it hard to imagine the world he was trying to paint for them. "Life was equally cheaper in those days. Today there is much money around, but it's like worthless paper, worthless coins. The amount of money we use for a bottle of King Size today was enough to provide one with a wife, a house and a good life for at least a year in the forties."

He smiled and shook his head dejectedly, as if in regret of missed opportunities.

"Things have changed, things have changed very much," he repeated. "And almost invariably for the worst."

"How I wish Tsanga were back here with me!" Dieudonné was almost in tears. There was a slight emotional tremor in his voice.

"I would feel supported and normal, reassured and happy despite my depression. But she's gone, and I feel so empty, so lonely," he regretted.

All of a sudden, he started to sing Pierre Tchana's 'San san boys': "Ma broda, if you like your wife, you must hold 'am fine. San san boy dem plenty. Dem go catch'am go …"

His glass was empty, but he didn't want to refill it just yet, so he put it down. Through with singing, he resumed his story.

"Before I met Tsanga four years ago, my only source of sexual satisfaction for forty years in Mimboland had been corner-corner love with the kick-and-pass women who hang about the bars and idle around the streets in Sawang, here, other big cities, and all over this beautiful country. Those you call 'Money-for-hand-back-for-down', 'Marché mondial', 'Station d'essence', 'Make-me-well', 'Weti-man-go-do', 'All-wata-di-quench-fire', and so on."

Margarita and the other women didn't particularly like the imagery, but they didn't stop him because they were experienced enough to know that what he said was factual, irrespective of how he said it. Convinced that Dieudonné meant no harm, they let him continue.

"It's extremely strange that my dear Tsanga should go away just like that," Dieudonné said ruefully. "She who was so fond of what she termed my bedroom eyes!" His female audience exchanged glances to say Tsanga was too generous, but did not interrupt him. "We loved each other to such a point that she was even ready to follow me back to Warzone! She was ready to venture into the unknown with me, to die by my side. But now she's vanished without a trace. What a shock!" He squeezed his eyes with his fingers to stop the tears while everyone watched him.

"Have you checked with her parents if she went to see them?" asked Dieumerci sympathetically.

"Of course," replied Dieudonné. "I've been to Nkola, her home village, to see her parents. But they don't seem to have seen her, though they aren't surprised by her behaviour. It appears that they are used to having their daughter run away from her husbands. What they found surprising, however, so they told me, was the fact that I've been able to keep Tsanga in one place for four whole years. Which to them was a telling sign that Tsanga must have loved me in a special way. So why did she run away? In what way have I wronged her beyond forgiveness? Haven't I always given her the best part of everything that has come my way? Why do you abandon me, Tsanga?" It was as if his beloved wife was there, listening to him.

"She was more than just a wife to me," he told his sympathetic listeners. "She was at the same time a mother, a sister and a friend to whom I could turn and share my sadness with, a container for my tears, she was. I miss her!" He cleaned his eyes with a handkerchief, which Margarita handed him.

"Before I left Warzone the first time, my father had found for me a beautiful young Arab girl by the name of Amina. Her parents hailed from the Arab north, and lived in Warzone City where they made charms and amulets, which they sold to people who sought protection against evil, misfortune and witchcraft, or who wanted to attract good luck, attention and love. When I married Amina, it was rumoured all over the village that her father had cast a spell on my father. The latter was an important man in our village, and it was Amina's father's ambition to cultivate close ties with everyone of importance in the neighbourhood, so the rumour went. Whether there was any truth in the rumour or not, I knew that my father paid the dowry and we took Amina along with us to Muzungu-Avenir 'pour défendre l'intérêt Muzungulandais' through the ruthless and savage slaughter of ordinary men, women and children who, tired of 'le meilleur du pire', had dared to tell Muzunguland: 'We need a bit of freedom'. I loved Amina very much, but I was a rough youth. In those crazy days, I used to beat her too often, and for very light offences. For example, I would beat her for drinking without my permission a Hamoud, my favourite drink in those days. Imagine, beating her up for drinking mere lemonade! She was good with extracting juice from the fruits of the baobab, to which she added water, sugar and sometimes powdered milk, vanilla and other flavourings. She also made minted juices from the leaves of the hibiscus, from the fruit of the tamarind, and from ginger. And not for anything in the world did I exchange my Hamoud for her Bouye, Bissap, Tamarind or Gingembre juices. This silly attitude of mine continued until she couldn't stand it any longer, and so she ran away back to her parents the very day we returned from Muzungu-Avenir. This must have accounted for why I drifted from the village into the arms of fate.

"Since then, I remained a bachelor until four years ago. When Tsanga came into my life, I thought I had at last a woman under whose comfort and care I was to spend whatever is still left of my life. Before meeting Tsanga, there was a tribes girl of mine who lived with her parents as refugees at Soum whom I came close to marrying. But just when I had finished paying the token prize, she eloped with a Wami youth."

He stole a look at Dieumerci, who felt slightly uneasy to belong to the same ethnic group as the young man who had eloped with Dieudonné's would-be wife. But there wasn't any remorse in Dieudonné's eyes. His look was more of an instinctive reaction than a conscious attempt to make any association.

"She wanted to forget Warzone totally and her compatriots whom she blamed indiscriminately for her tribulations," Dieudonné carried on. "She wouldn't reason with me when I tried to explain to her that the majority of her compatriots were innocent victims of a conflict they didn't understand themselves. Only a handful of mean madmen driven by greed were causing us all this trouble! Anyway, that's how I missed Fatimata, as she was called, beautiful and lovely just like the Fatimata Sam Mangwana sings about, and just as jealous: 'Fatimata ma belle, ta façon d'aimer, ce pas jolie, ce pas gentille. Ta façon d'aimer, Jaloue, Jaloue ...' I haven't seen her since, but I know that her parents eventually passed away as was reported by *radio trottoir*. Fatimata is probably somewhere doing business with her Wami husband. I wish them luck," he said without bitterness, then sang *Fatimata* for a while, accompanied by those who knew the song like him.

What Dieudonné did not add was his initial bitterness with Fatimata for turning him down for a Mimbolander. He had described her as "ready to use and be used in order to survive the traumas of war", something that had hurt her terribly. With hindsight, he had regretted his selfish and inconsiderate remarks, but had not found her to apologise.

"I have never asked and will never ask a woman with whom I'm staying to leave me, Insha'Allah," said Dieudonné, contemplating the white handkerchief in his hand. "All wata di quench fire, no be so? House wey yi catch fire di know dorti wata?"

Some men laughed, some women frowned, but Dieudonné meant no harm.

"Only a woman can reject or abandon me for reasons of her own," he sounded depressed again. "Perhaps because I'm poor and know nothing. But I take everything the way it comes, and place Allah at the forefront of all I do, think or say. I've never dreamt of polygamy, because I'm too poor. As for the rich, it's perhaps a good idea for them to have two wives. The one can help the other in case of illness or when there is too much work to do at home.

Apart from which reason, polygamy in itself has no raison d'être pour moi." He tried to smile, but didn't succeed because his heart was in a state of gloom.

"Before Tsanga's sudden disappearance, it was my idea to take her for medical examination at l'Hôpital Populaire."

He accidentally dropped the handkerchief, but Dieumerci quickly picked it up and handed it back to him. Dieudonné mumbled his thanks and continued.

"Despite her age, she was never tired of hoping for a child with me. She believed that her father, however much he tried to hide the fact, had cursed her following the failure of her first marriage, and especially after the mysterious death of Atangana, their only grandchild. She kept mourning that a woman who cannot bear children is like a river that has dried up. Now that she is gone with the money I've been saving, I only wish she realises it wasn't for myself, but for her own good that I stored the money away under the mattress. With her gone, my nostalgia for Warzone and for my mother and sisters increases with each new day." He suddenly started singing Prince Nico Mbarga's celebrated *Sweet Mother*:

Sweet Mother I no go forget you, for the suffer wey you suffer for me so …

> If I no chop you no go chop …
> If I no sleep you no go sleep …
> If di cry …

He danced to the song seated, and the others joined in the singing. Then Chopngomna ordered Precious to play the record, and the dance floor was busy until *Sweet Mother* had run its course.

"How I wish I had the money to make real this dream!" Dieudonné resumed, mopping his face. "I would go straight back home and see for myself what is actually the matter between Musa and Hassan, the warlords of Warzone. But I leave all for Allah the Almighty to decide." He clasped his hands prayerfully and looked up at the ceiling for a while, noticing lizards and wasps crossing rafters effortlessly, making him wish borders were that easy to tame. If only he had the freedom of a bird …

"I still remember the first day I met Tsanga. What can be more vivid in a man's mind than his first meeting with the woman he loves? It was right here at the Grand Canari, and my favourite tune by Anne Marie Nzie, the one I danced to a while ago, was playing. There she appeared at the entrance of the bar – an accomplished beauty, average height, and well-built – a woman to whom Allah had been truly generous! I gazed at her with young eyes of age and told her: 'Beauty, you are pretty. Will you make my day? I have nothing to offer but poverty, guaranteed. But I promise you won't regret a thing.' My smile touched her heart and she smiled back like the gatekeeper of my destiny. I said: 'Welcome to poverty.' And she said: 'I have seen worse.' I offered her a drink, knowing there and then, that I had a wife. When you meet the right person, it clicks in a special way even when you are drunk."

The others nodded.

"There and then she warned: 'I hope you are not going to be like the evil swine I've just left. Two years of marriage to the bastard have been total hell. Day in and day out, I wake up at night just to find someone on me going zic-zic-zic. I don't know what it is like to have a good time. Le salaud, even when I'm sleeping, he climbs on me, he doesn't seek my opinion. J'ai l'impression que pour lui, je suis un objet. It is only when I venture out with someone else that it dawns on me that love making can be fun. Il me caresse, il me touche, j'ai l'impression que je compte pour lui …'"

"'Chérie, your nightmares are over', I reassured her with a kiss and a drink. Later on that night I proved myself amply," Dieudonné laughed. "A man is what a man can do," he added uneasily. Only he knew the truth of his claims.

"That day, before coming here to Grand Canari, I had drunk enough Munding Swine Quarter, unsure as I was, to be greeted with generous offers of King Size. Perhaps some of you call me this nickname without knowing what it means."

He paused and took a brief look round the bar, as if to ask those who didn't know to own up. But he didn't do that. Instead, he laughed a dry laugh, and continued.

"I was nicknamed Munding Swine Quarter because, instead of our popular thick, cloudy, local grain beer that fills one up like food, I used to drink so much of the local gin that was brewed and still continues to be brewed, though to a lesser degree, here in Swine Quarter. The gin, as you know, can turn your eyes one hundred times more than can Muzungulander gin. But it is a thousand times cheaper. The gin was so strong that some people used it to make fire when there was no kerosene. That is how strong the gin was, but because I took so much, it was like drinking water – Munding. It's a drink with over two hundred names. The most famous of them here in Mimboland are Arki, L'Alcool du Pays, Mambala, Bessala, Man-Pass-Man, Ajousalcafala and Cent Degrés. In Warzone, we have Kachasu, Sodabi and Gongo. Further south, the common ones are Waragi, Chang'aa, Katikala, and Akpeteshie. Ogogoro, Kaikai, Sumsum, Ataya, and Afofo, are much more popular west of here. I drank this gin non-stop for twenty-three years. Then I was a real drunkard, a notorious one who used to enter and win drinking competitions on this gin that was officially banned but secretly allowed. For such competitions, Omo was added to make the gin even stronger, and if I could still stand up after winning, the brewing women who provided for the competition would insist I ate pepper soup to wash everything down. Then my lips and my intestines were truly on fire. Those were the days when Dieudonné was Dieudonné. But my rate of drinking has drastically dropped. Everything seems to die with age. Those who have known me for a long time would confirm when I say that I no longer drink as much as I used to. Munding is an exceedingly powerful gin when brewed by an expert, of which there are still a few around. It's brewed from water, palm wine, cassava, banana, sugar cane, cashew, maize, millet or sorghum. In this section of Swine Quarter where we are sitting, are two specialist women brewers of Munding. However well they brew today, they can't do it with the perfection of brewers of those early years, one must admit. It was simply perfect! When I drank a litre or two of Munding, I felt like someone in flames though unlike in my early years of bubbly youth I never did anything to harm anyone," Dieudonné added in a lower tone, realising they had only his word for it.

"Though Monsieur and Madame Toubaaby accuse me of drinking too much, I don't drink more than most people," Dieudonné pointed out. "The question I always put to whoever accuses me of drinking too much is to know whether I drink more than everyone else in Mimboland. If I'm attacked or assaulted when drunk, my most common reaction is to weep. I weep because I'm sorry for myself. I don't understand why anyone should treat others in a way he wouldn't like to be treated. I never think of beating somebody even if I could, because to do that is to beat myself as well. For sure he feels pain when I beat him, and so do I."

Dieumerci interrupted Dieudonné with an offer of another bottle of King Size. This time Chopngomna the cheerful supplier didn't move to stop or humiliate him again. Instead he smiled his appreciation to Dieumerci and even wanted to add to the offer, but Margarita stopped him, saying: "Allow Dieudonné to terminate his interesting story, then he can drink as much as he likes *on me*." She stressed the last two words.

Dieudonné beckoned Precious, who came and uncapped the beer for him. He took a gulp and cleared his throat to resume his story. But just when he was about to begin, Dieumerci interrupted him again.

"What would you do if the government were suddenly to place a ban on the production of alcohol?" Dieumerci asked with a smile.

"If the government decides to stop the production of alcohol," began Dieudonné in a low voice, "I'd drink water and thank Allah the Almighty for it." He paused for a moment. Then he added, "But it would be silly for the government to do a crazy thing like that. I am no big book, but everyone knows that alcohol solves a lot of political and social problems, economic ones as well. And the government should know this more than anyone else. Alcohol is used at birthday parties, marriage ceremonies, to celebrate appointments and promotions, and at death ceremonies to say farewell to lost ones. Stranger buyers and native sellers of land here in Nyamandem use *vin rouge* – the famous fivelitre Cassanova that can recharge any battery however flat – for their transactions – the buyer ensuring that the seller is fed enough Cassanova to stop him from overcharging. Even priests can't say Mass without a bit of *vin de messe*. Not to mention those whose lives revolve around parties, both social and political. When one is most downcast or overwhelmed by daily financial, domestic and other problems, one resorts to alcohol to avoid the more drastic alternative of suicide or political violence. So, it would be foolish and dangerous for the government to dare to ban such a functional and all-purpose thing. And, in any case, aren't the most prosperous breweries in Mimboland owned by members of government, President Longstay himself heading the list?

"Mimbo sabi do kan kan thing for all kana people. Beer makes some aggressive and dangerous towards others. Mais, we must mimba say aggression and danger dey, bière or no bière. So mimbo dey like door wey yi fit open all side – to the left and to the right, up and down. For some alcohol is there to calm them, for ara one, mimbo fit make them wake up like fire… Bing! Bing! Like manpikin stan'up!" He pointed to the colourful ad of a dark couple on the wall advertising Whisky Black with the words: 'As powerful as the men who drink it.'

They all burst out laughing at Dieudonné's style, and not in doubt of the veracity of his views. It was true that alcohol served different ends to different consumers, and even non-consumers. Some drink to warm up, some to cool down, others to forget they should not be drinking. Some may not themselves drink, but they use alcohol purposefully. Those who are drunk need alcohol as clearance, and those who have experienced a sudden shock need it to steady their nerves. Some drink because they are unemployed, others to forget the pressures and boredom of work; some to celebrate happiness, others to cushion the burdens of despair; some to keep busy, others to keep idle; some to contest, others to condone. In some, alcohol induces feelings of bonhomie, in others hunger for violence and vengeance. Husbands drink for courage to start a quarrel with wives and divert attention from their failure to provide for their families while wives drink to challenge failing husbands. Whatever the reason for taking alcohol, as he had put it, "such a move by the government would amount to biting the very finger that keeps you in power. L'alcool tue la violence politique. And the government is no fool."

"No be I hear say Masa President he sepsep don give order say make all people for Mimboland open bar for all corner for Mimboland?" Dieudonné asked rhetorically.

Margarita agreed. "That's right. The government has made it very easy to start a business in alcohol. The President recently declared, if you apply to open a school, it takes time and don't you dare go ahead until government approval is granted. But if you apply for permission to start an off-licence bar and do not get a reply after two weeks of formal deposition of your application, go right ahead. Silence is consent."

"That makes sense," Dieumerci came in. "According to statistics by breweries collected by a friend of mine researching on the names people give drinking places, the number of bars in Nyamandem has increased from 3,002 to 4,500 in under two years. And that is not counting hundreds of circuits, chicken parlours and other unlicensed drinking places where alcohol and food are sold round the clock."

"You see!" stressed Margarita, parting her hair stylishly. "Government's goal is to have beer within an arm's reach of desire in every neighbourhood, every town, every village."

Dieudonné thanked her and added, "And there is more, as you know. These days when the stench of poverty is everywhere, if the 'mange mille' police or gendarmes find fault with a taxi driver's car or documents, they would rather accept a winning beer cap than let go a driver who has no money to bribe them." He was referring to the proliferation of promotions by breweries luring Mimbolanders with hidden prizes under the bottle caps of the beers competing for their attention.

"In fact, the other day someone was on the radio explaining how increasingly Mimbolanders in the big cities are using beer bottle caps as currency, and wondering if this was not a threat to normal money," Dieumerci came in, impressed at how informed Dieudonné was.

"I guard my winning caps jealously," said Dieudonné, searching his back trouser pockets for two King Size winning caps, which he showed off proudly. "With one of these, whether you good people are around or not to be generous, I am sure of a King Size," he laughed. "There are days I am as lucky as hell. I come here with nothing in my pockets, ask Precious timidly to uncap a King Size for me, and before I open my mouth to say I am drinking on credit, I win, and win, and win, and can drink, drink and drink, and at times, I go home with a couple more free bottles, thanks to winning caps. We must be grateful to the beer companies for giving away millions of free beer!"

Everyone laughed heartily.

"But I am not that lucky since I am yet to win a mobile phone, a television and a car, which are also on offer," Dieudonné added, his eyes smilingly on Chopngomna, who was lying about his whereabouts into one of his mobile phones.

"Mobile phone and television maybe, but I gather the cars are not easy to win even when they are won since the managers of the breweries always ensure that the winning cap goes to someone close to them. It is rumoured the manager of a leading brewery in Sawang lost his job when his girlfriend came to the brewery with a winning cap for a car promotion that was never launched." Bonblanc Mukala Ni-Ni interjected, emptying the contents of a 'whisky condom' into a glass half full with Casanova, his eyes as unsteady as a butterfly pregnant with indecision. His cracked lips quivered as his women competed to freshen them with kisses.

"That may be so, but some people actually do win the cars," Margarita countered. "The other day I read in *The Mimbolander Post* about a young mechanic who won a Citroën C4 from uncapping his very first Gold Harp ever. Can you imagine? That's what we call luck!" she exclaimed.

Dieudonné made known he wasn't complaining when he said his luck was limited. "I'm happy with the beer I win, the taxi men are happy with theirs, and so are the policemen who snatch winning caps from them to turn a blind eye at their traffic offences. In any case, mobile phones are much too unsafe in my neighbourhood. From thieves to pit latrines, everyone is desperate for one. The other day, a young woman was cursing herself and inviting some boys to help retrieve her mobile phone from a stinking latrine filled with maggots. She could hear it ring when her number was called, but no boy was willing to stick his head into maggot-infested excrement for a fee. Not so long ago, another Swine Quarter resident forgot his mobile phone on the counter of a store, went back shortly afterwards, and the store boy swore the man never left any phone behind. Desperate, the man asked a friend to call his number, only to hear his phone ringing inside the socks worn by the very same store boy! Allah teaches us to be grateful for the little mercies of life."

"J'ai la constipation des oreilles," Chopngomna announced, drying his tears of joy. "With Dieudonné to make me laugh and cry, who needs to go to the movies?" This was in response to Margarita, who had just reminded him that there was a 3 pm movie – Charlie Chaplin's *The Great Dictator* – showing at Cinema du Muzunguland, which they shouldn't miss. As a civil servant, he didn't need reminding that dictatorship was the biggest tree in Mimboland's political jungle. A well-known satirical comedian had caught the attention of the killer squad for daring to say in public: 'Like woman, President Longstay na elephant meat. You di chop'am yi no di finish.'

To humour her, Chopngomna told Margarita, "Chérie, your eyes! When you look at me this way, I could drown in your bedroom eyes just like that."

Margarita pretended not to hear him. Instead, she volunteered to fetch some roasted meat from a nearby vendor, on condition that Dieudonné was held on pause. Smiling in anticipation of something to hold the King Size in check in his stomach, Dieudonné promised not to say a word until Margarita was back. Instead, he asked for another tune, Pierre Tchana's 'Rien n'a changé', which he followed with nostalgia.

CHAPTER TWELVE

Dieudonné ate in a way that betrayed him. Drinking on an empty stomach is ill-advised, especially for seasoned drinkers. But without Tsanga at home to see to it that he ate regularly, he was allowing a disturbing imbalance between food and drink. And this was telling on his person and appetite.

"You have spoken well," said Dieumerci, when Dieudonné had finished eating the roasted meat (a mixture of red beef, crushed genitals – *mbangala* – and entrails variously and popularly known as bible, towel, exhaust pipe and roundabout) Margarita brought him. "But just for a change of topic," he went on, "could you tell us more about the animals for which you work? I really would like to know how many times a day you feed them, how you prepare their food, how often you bathe them, and so on. I'm most intrigued," concluded Dieumerci, getting even closer to Dieudonné, who was fingering his few surviving teeth for stuck shreds of beef, and rinsing everything down with gulps of King Size.

"I'm here to tell you my life story as I promised to. But it is impossible to remember all that has ever happened to me, or even to tell you all that I remember. However, every question that you pose for which I have an answer, I'm going to do my best to satisfy you, Insha'Allah," Dieudonné assured. Then he insinuated, "I don't know why you intellectuals are so inquisitive, but I know that I have to satisfy your curiosity since I promised to. Since you have asked to know about the animals, I'll tell you about the animals."

Dieumerci was delighted. He wanted to know about the Toubaabys beyond their scholarship, and no one was better placed than Dieudonné to zoom an inquisitive lens into their private sphere.

"For one dog and eight cats, Monsieur and Madame Toubaaby spend over MIM$100,000 a month on food alone. These nine animals are like children to the couple. Like me, they don't have any children of their own. Once I overheard Madame telling her friend why she does not have children. She said: 'When I was young and wanted children, my husband was too busy studying. And when he had finished studying and wanted children, I was too busy studying. And now that we have both finished studying, we are too old to dare.' Lucky people! I've been searching for a child with a torch all my life, flinging right and flinging left, and still nothing comes my way, not even by accident. I've fired blanks all my life, like a eunuch. And to imagine them making such light choices!" Dieudonné sounded angry.

Madame Toubaaby's reason for not having children reminded Dieumerci of something he had read recently on a man of power lamenting: 'When I was young I loved booze but couldn't afford it. Now it's all free but the doctor says I can't touch it.' Dieumerci shook his head thinking: The ironies of life! But whatever sympathy he had for the man had disappeared with a damning indictment of him in the same newspaper: 'When he was president, he never used to look down. His head was always turned towards the skies. Why? He didn't want to see the hardship on the faces of his people. Looking at the faces was likely to create sympathy for the people, which of course he didn't want. If you don't look at my face, how would you know I have problems?'

"When Monsieur and Madame go on a visit to Muzunguland, they leave me behind with elaborate instructions on how to take care of these precious creatures – when and what to cook for them, how to clean them, what soap to use, how to turn on the air-conditioner when it is too hot for them, and so on. It's not uncommon for Madame to make an unexpected visit to Muzunguland because one of her darlings has fallen ill. Not so long ago she took two of her cats to Muzunguland for a thorough medical examination and treatment. Both animals happened to have lost appetite for some days and she felt very worried about their health. In Muzunguland, they were hospitalised for two weeks until they regained their health. Every one of these animals has a doctor of its own back home in Muzunguland who studies their medical records meticulously and regularly – for Madame who pays them quite well."

"A doctor!" screamed someone. Others followed suit. They were stunned by what Dieudonné had just said. It was incredible to imagine cats with doctors of their own when they knew doctors to belong to one of the most underrepresented professions in Mimboland. They were incredulous of Dieudonné's claims since some of them had never been to a doctor before, not for want of trying. But he was honest, presenting things as he saw them. If they had the misfortune not to have doctors and adequate medical care, that was no reason to disbelieve that elsewhere cats and dogs had doctors to take good care of them. So he insisted.

"Yes, a doctor," he affirmed. "Each of these animals has a doctor of its own. Why do you think Madame always takes them to Muzunguland in sickness? I still remember an instance when the most beloved of all the cats got caught in a trap and lost its leg. Believe it or not, the cat was immediately rushed to the airport and evacuated to Muzunguland for emergency medical care. There in Muzunguland, the leg was amputated by a specialist doctor."

Dieudonné looked at his listeners, disbelief was written on their faces. He couldn't blame them for that. He understood perfectly their position. Had he not worked for white men all his life, and had he not been personally involved, he equally would have found his story hard to swallow. When Dieudonné insisted, they allowed him to carry on with his tale, though this didn't mean that he had convinced them.

"They take high quality meals. I use water from the filter to cook their food. Perhaps you may be pleased to know Monsieur and Madame don't drink pipe-borne water either. They prefer mineral water, carefully bottled and sealed – 'L'eau des Dieux' as we call it

– in the absence of which they go for rain water harvested directly from the skies, which still they must boil and filter to eliminate germs." Dieudonné volunteered the information that his listeners found too obvious. If animals could discriminate between the type of water to drink, how much more of their masters? So they just nodded with understanding, and he continued with his tale.

"The animals eat lots of different kinds of food," he said. "They eat fish, Uncle Ben's rice and macaroni from Muzunguland, and natural fruit from the Mimboland Development Corporation. They also eat canned food supplements that Madame purchases in big supermarkets such as Score, Bon Marché, and Prix Unique. When I started working for them, Madame gave me an orientation course for two weeks, during which time I learnt to cook all over again. Cooking for animals is not like cooking for you and me, I was told. Animals are more delicate beings and need highly balanced diets, Madame kept repeating. When finally she was satisfied with my grasp of the theory, Madame sent me to the kitchen to practice. But for the two days that followed, she watched me closely, with the same critical impatience that the Muzungulander colonial masters watched their political criminals among the Warzone peasantry." Dieudonné shook his head in self-pity.

"Each of those animals has separate plates and dishes," he made his story even more fabulous. "They have nothing in common with the dogs and cats we know in our villages and around Swine Quarter. The dog, for instance, isn't like the typical village dog born and bred in poverty that fends for itself, and that survives on excrement and kitchen waste. Cats around here as we know are kept largely so that they might help us win the war against the rats that destroy valuable things in our perforated houses. But Monsieur and Madame rear their animals to the point of adoration. And the animals are more disciplined than some of us. I swear. They know when to eat, when to sleep and when to make love. A male cat would say, 'Now, now' and the female, if not in the mood, would reply, 'Not now, not now.'" He imitated the mew of the cat.

The audience roared with laughter, and Dieudonné seized the opportunity to wet his lips with a gulp of King Size. All eyes were on him as his story stretched their credulity even further.

"My experiences have made me sensitive to such a point that I start to weep if I see someone crying. No one ever cries for nothing. Heavy problems hide behind the tears we shed. Would you imagine that cooking for these animals as I do, Madame never allows me to taste the food I prepare? If I'm forbidden to taste what I cook, how do I know that there is enough salt? That the balance is right? Is it poison that I've prepared to eliminate the animals that I can't taste lest I die along with them? But I never mind. No worries. I commit my life entirely to Allah the Almighty, who must have a purpose for making a beggar of me in a world of plenty. As fruits of Allah's creation with a part to play in his grand design of things, either we are begging, stealing or being rewarded accordingly." He was philosophical.

"What is more," he continued with his tale of animals placed above his humanity, "I'm not even allowed to eat what may remain of the animals' meals. She wouldn't even let me lick up what her lovely little darlings have spat out. Sometimes I'm so hungry that I ask Madame for a little to eat. But invariably, she asks why I fail to bring my own food to eat at work. I must say, though, that once in a blue moon, she amazes me with the rare offer of something to eat. Generally, Monsieur is slightly better in his treatment of me. He is the better of the two lovely devils. Once in a while, he gives me a cup of tea and a slice of bread." Dieudonné caressed his beardless chin over and over, his mind deep in thought, and his empty drinking-glass gazing at him from the floor.

"Sometimes, I'm forced to shed tears when Madame uses harsh language on me," said Dieudonné, slowly, more to himself than to his eager audience.

Much louder, he added, "She often accuses me of drunkenness and makes me look like a little child in front of her. I've asked her many times if back home in Muzunguland children don't have any respect for their grandfathers. But she never answers this question. Instead, she prefers to ask me why a full bottle of beer in the store suddenly and unaccountably becomes empty. There are provocative questions like this which make me to weep like a child."

He was again depressed. Sudden bouts of depression were a strange characteristic of his. Others couldn't understand why the emotions of happiness and sadness were so interwoven in his person. Why couldn't he have a moment's happiness without being reminded of his sad experiences as well?

Meanwhile Dieudonné continued, almost as if by compulsion to fulfil the promise of telling his story to the end.

"I can stay for hours without alcohol, but I find it difficult not to smoke, a dirty habit I picked up at Muzungu-Avenir" Dieudonné confessed, oblivious to the conspiracy alcohol and cigarettes had ignited against his health. He was a tall man by nature, but he had not always been slim and frail, like an underfed tree in the heart of a strong storm. His lungs were at the mercy of his smoking, and his liver far more corrupted by alcohol than he could imagine. But his strength was the fact that he didn't know any of this and wouldn't care even if he knew. As he would say, 'Un petit n'est pas un grand'.

"When I drink I feel fine, but if I fail to smoke, I'm full of bile. I become so wicked and bitter. At such moments, I'm tempted to retort to Madame, or to address her harshly in return. I may even refuse to answer when she speaks but this doesn't make matters any easier. It only adds to my problems because in consequence, I'm accused of rudeness or insolence. What I would like to know is why for five years Madame persists in accusing me of drunkenness when I don't behave like a drunkard any more than do others. I've never stayed away from work for more than a day, not even in sickness. Is that the characteristic of a drunkard? Don't non-drinkers fall sick, or stay away from work for one reason or another? I might drink, but I'm always conscious of what I do, and especially of my job. If I were a drunkard as Madame so hotly claims, why doesn't she ever allow me the dregs of the drinks in the glasses of her guests? She prefers to throw these dregs away if Flic isn't in the mood to intoxicate himself."

"Who is Flic?" interrupted Chopngomna, all excited.

Dieudonné looked up at the generous giver and smiled, pleased as usual to know that his story was interesting. He seized the opportunity to ask for a cigarette. One of the other men readily offered to buy him a packet of Minty at MIM$100. Dieudonné was thrilled and again took up his story. This time, he smoked and drank as he spoke.

"I thought I told you that the giant frightful watchdog is called Flic," said he, feigning surprise. "It's the real night watch in that compound. Its bark and howl are terrifying, and actually make the blood go cold in the veins of every visitor. Onguene, the night watchman, whose brains are as empty as he is bald, would be incapable of a thing without Flic. For one thing, Onguene is half deaf, and for another, he sleeps like a corpse. One night, Monsieur and Madame decided to test his sense of alertness. They connected an alarm to the store where Onguene slept. Madame set the bell ringing while Monsieur observed Onguene. But there was no reaction. Onguene continued to sleep, snoring and groaning like a pig. The Toubaabys didn't send him away, though. I suppose they thought it suffices to know that there is a night watchman for a thief to keep his distance, even if the night watchman is a corpse like Onguene. The Toubaabys have been assaulted and stolen from only once. That was before Onguene was employed. At first, Monsieur and Madame had thought they could do without a night watchman, believing their electric fence protection to be enough.

But when they missed death just by a hair's breadth, they decided upon further security – a human presence. I think that Onguene is merely paid for spending his nights away from his wife, and for keeping Flic busy at night with his shoes that smell like rotten eggs. That's all the work he does! Unlike other night watchmen that I have known, he always has a full night's sleep!"

Dieudonné's humour made everyone laugh.

"Can you tell us more about the cats?" asked Margarita. "How did the couple come to possess so many cats? Tell us more," she implored.

"Women are the same everywhere," commented one of the men. "What does she want to know more about the cats for?"

"Probably to acquire her own, isn't it chérie?" replied Chopngomna, embracing Margarita. He was half serious, half joking. The fact that Margarita was aggressively buying into Muzungulander cultural values, especially the new consumer dimensions of being Muzungulander, worried him at times – not so much because of the extra demands on his wallet but because of the mimicry it brought about, making his otherwise beautiful, elegant and dignified Margarita appear ludicrously devalued and idiotic in her imitativeness. Sometimes he wondered, in amusement, of course, what would be left of Margarita if she were really to strip to only what God had endowed her with at birth, as even the hair, finger and toe nails she was wearing would have to come off, given that these were all additives, externally grafted beautifiers borrowed from dead Muzungulander women. Through her craving for attachments, she and other Mimbolander women contributed to ensuring that no Muzungulander woman would be dead and buried for good.

"I'll tell you about the cats if that's what you want to hear," Dieudonné reassured Margarita, who didn't particularly appreciate the preceding remarks, and who, instead of retorting, opted to wet her lips with more red lipstick, assisted by a pocket mirror.

"They are eight in number as I told you. The elderly white one is the mother of all the others. These cats would have been far more than their present number, if Madame had wanted. But she was interested in the best cats only, which explains why she carried out a sort of selection exercise. The mother has put to birth three times. The first time she brought forth six kittens, but only one of them survived the selection test. The rejected five were simply killed and buried behind the big fence. The second time the white mother again delivered six – three white and three black kittens. In this instance, four lucky ones were selected for life – three Toubaaby and one black. The two others followed the fate of their unfortunate predecessors. The third time the white mother was taken to Muzunguland for fear of complicated birth. It is also because Madame wanted it to be her last. This time it was a caesarean birth to only two kittens, both of which were satisfactory to Madame. Among the eight cats are three male ones, which have all been castrated." Dieudonné couldn't resist a chuckle, as his story sounded much like a joke to everyone.

"Madame has lots of books on cats, but her favourite is a beautiful book in colour: *Les Chats: Photographies et Poèmes*, which she never tires of showing her visitors, or anyone with a minute to spare. From this book, she has chosen a favourite poem to go with each of her cats. The poem about her black cat, she reads aloud to her Muzungulander visitors or to herself so often that I have come to know the poem off by heart: 'Dark in the dark. Darker than darkness. Darker than blacks fighting at midnight in a cave. To disappear, I don't need to hide myself; I simply cease to exist and I switch off my headlights. Even better, I put my golden headlights away under the carpet, floating in the air, visible and impossible to grap, and I turn to my business… Is it magic? But of course. Do you think one can be this dark without being a wizard?' At the end of every recitation, she and her visitors would explode in laughter, and praise the composer of the poem – a certain 'Colette Autres

Bêtes' – possibly her fellow Muzungulander." He paused to take a gulp. "Strange woman," he whispered.

"Unlike ghetto cats which survive only on mice, Madame hates any of her cats to eat cheap. There is no doubt that Madame loves her animals dearly," he became serious again. "A friend of Madame's, a fellow white lady, came and begged for one of the cats – the one called Blondie. Madame accepted and her friend took the cat away. The following morning, as I came to work, I met Madame weeping at the entrance. I was stunned. I had never known that such a tough woman could shed a tear. Monsieur had gone on a research trip, so Madame was alone. At first I thought that my presence might make her stop weeping. But she continued to weep, curse and threaten. I asked her what the matter was. She told me the story of how it all happened, and how now she missed her lovely cat badly. She told me how she didn't have the courage to go back to her friend's and collect 'Blondie, Blondie ma chérie, mon étoile'. I advised her to stop crying and go for her beloved Blondie. She pulled herself together, got into the car and drove to her friend's. Half an hour later she came back smiling. In the car with her was dear Blondie. Madame was ecstatic. She called out to me: 'Dieudonné, Dieudonné, venez voir. Je l'ai fait! J'ai ramené ma chérie, ma Blondie!' So I went and saw. She was extremely happy. I had never seen her that happy. She said: 'Dieudonné, vous savez, souvent les bêtes sont bien meilleur que les hommes.' She actually said that sometimes one's best friend is an animal and often one's worst enemy is a man. I'm not lying. Slowly and heavily, I turned and walked down to the kitchen, my mind deep in thought, to cook for Blondie and the rest of Madame's dear friends," Dieudonné concluded with clouded eyes.

"During that brief mutiny and attempted coup that took place two years ago, Madame and Monsieur were both on holiday in Muzunguland. I was left alone in Beverly Hills to take care of their big residence. Whenever they travel out of Nyamandem, they ask me to come and stay at their palace and look after the animals and other delicate property of theirs. I must assure you that during the three days that the war lasted, when thousands of bullets smuggled in from Muzunguland in sardine cans perforated buildings, making victims everywhere, what I went through was worse than hell! Nothing to eat, no water to drink either! Ambitious rebels who wanted to seize power and form their own government cut off all supplies for three days. There was no electricity during that time. Everywhere there was nothing but darkness. Beverly Hills, for whatever reason, was particularly targeted by the rebels, some of whom implanted themselves at strategic corners listening into their radios for instructions.

"For once, I didn't care about the dog and the cats, and convinced myself that my life was more important. I stole a bit of their fish and milk, which I ate and drank for survival. You must know that it was an awful experience, a matter of life and death! But I survived. The animals survived, too, and I was happy they did. Finally, only Tsanga's whereabouts and situation were unknown, thus keeping me worried. I didn't believe I was going to find her alive again. She had been forced to stay away from me by the bloody skirmishes. But she, too, came out of it safe and sound. Allah is great." Dieudonné cleaned his face with the handkerchief he still held in his hand. Then he carefully folded it again, following the original folds. Satisfied that his handkerchief was neatly folded, Dieudonné placed it on his knee and supported it with an elbow.

"After the war, the Toubaabys returned to Mimboland," he resumed. "Madame was the first to arrive from the airport. She rapped impatiently at the gate. I went to unlock it and to welcome her. 'Soyez le bienvenue, Madame' I told her, with the respectfulness of the servant that I am. But she didn't answer. She appeared not to have heard, so I repeated the greeting. Then she said, 'Haah' with impatience and annoyance. So I knew that she was simply not interested in my welcome wish. It appeared there was something else, which alone was going to determine whether she was welcome or not. She seized the bunch of keys from me and opened the main door into their mansion. Then she went in and stood at the centre of the parlour with hands akimbo, calling for her animals one by one, each by name." He took a quick gulp.

"First came Flic, the dog. It wagged its tail and jumped around her. She stopped to embrace it and allowed it to lick her nose and lips. I winced at the sight of it, but Madame loved every second of the contact. When she was through with kissing and being kissed by Flic, Madame called Antoinette, the mother of the seven other cats. Antoinette was delighted to see her mistress and friend after a long separation. She mewed several times and was embraced and kissed in the same manner that Flic was. After Antoinette came Marx, followed by Richelieu, Blondie, Sartre, Claudine-Françoise, Gigi, and Leloup. As these animals came up one by one for inspection and cuddles, Madame's face brightened with reassurance. After the inspection that brought her satisfaction, she turned to me, her accusing eyes piercing, and said: 'Dieudonné, when we were leaving for Muzunguland, I forgot the key to the cupboard in which I store wine and whisky. Tell me what you drank from it.' They have some of the best collections of wines and whiskies from Muzunguland, the sort much craved after by the high and mighty of Mimboland, and which elite status-seekers are likely to offer their bosses for instant visibility.

"Her question sent my mind spinning. It filled me with anguish, bitterness and self-pity. For half a minute, I was lost in a concoction of queer emotions. There was Madame, who knew all that had happened in the country in their absence. Suppose, just suppose the rebellious soldiers had broken into the compound and wrecked everything, killing me as well and emptying her cupboard and house of all its contents. What would she have done upon her return from Muzunguland? Now that I have stayed locked up in their compound to take care of their house, their animals and all their property, she asks me a silly question about what I dared to drink from her rich wine cupboard. That is how I thought, and the more the thought persisted, the more bitter I felt. However, I mastered myself and told her simply that I drank a little wine during my three-day ordeal when I had no food to eat and no water to drink. Again, I couldn't resist being bitter as I told her this. What would this lady have done if I had acted like a thief by evacuating their house and escaping with all their property? Did she stop to think at all before opening her mouth? I wondered if she ever reflected. She is really a strange type, Madame Toubaaby, bizarre," Dieudonné was still as puzzled as he was then. He failed to add that that was the day he contemplated suicide for the first time, only to realise that when you are born in this world, you have to live in it. Sometimes your application to die is rejected repeatedly for no apparent reason.

Feeling Dieudonné's exhaustion, Chopngomna mobilised his generosity once again: "Serve our good storyteller friend a bowl of pepper soup and plantains," he ordered Precious. "And add the bill to the rest of what I have to settle." He sounded as extravagant as the well-connected civil servant that he was.

Dieudonné, who was increasingly at the mercy of alcohol, thanked Chopngomna for his timely offer. Dieumerci snatched the opportunity to rush out for a sandwich of the entrails of a cow, and also to consult his notebook for any outstanding questions, but gave up on the entrails when a wretched boy, obviously offended by the person selling, screamed: "Best best entrails. Come one, come all. Chop shit. A million flies can't be wrong!" The seller was doing everything to chase the boy and the flies away. "You no well! You sense don go waka!" the seller screamed at the boy, holding out his knife.

Picturing a typical day in the life of a ghetto fly, Dieumerci held his hunger in check and returned to the bar despite the seller's attempts to reassure him: "Nos mouches sont stérilisées".

Dieumerci was just in time to catch the tail end of what the flowery albino, Bonblanc Mukala Ni-Ni, who had listened to Dieudonné patiently, was telling the amazed audience about how the Mimboland Minister of Culture and National Heritage had taken a journalist to court for daring to report about a recent sumptuous high profile party the minister had thrown to celebrate the first anniversary of his cat.

"Birthday party for his cat?" Chopngomna asked in disbelief.

"Yes, C-A-T" Bonblanc Mukala Ni-Ni spelt out. "And its daily budget is five times higher than the salary of a chief of service at the ministry he heads," Bonblanc Mukala Ni-Ni added.

CHAPTER THIRTEEN

It is not because a horse is willing that one should ride it to death. If even Dieudonné's masters had failed in that, not for want of trying – it must be qualified as he would – Dieumerci knew better than to ride the race of death with Dieudonné. But as another saying goes, appetite grows with eating, especially for those who have made a creed of greed. Dieumerci had convinced himself that there were aspects of Dieudonné's life he absolutely wanted to know, driven by the very same selfish academic reasons that had brought them to the Grand Canari. Anxious not to be labelled *cochon académique* by the demanding Professor Toubaaby, Dieumerci was ready to risk tasking the willing horse just a mile further.

"Dieudonné, I see that you're very exhausted," said Dieumerci. "But I would like to ask you a very last question," he requested.

"Go right ahead," replied Dieudonné. "But let this be the very last as you say, for I'd like to go home for a deep sleep." He yawned. "Today I would like to go to bed with the sun."

Turning to Chopngomna the generous supplier, Dieudonné said, "I appreciate all you've done and are still prepared to do, but there comes a time when even I must say no to King Size. I wish I could stay for much longer, but I don't want to be late for work tomorrow, particularly as I've been severely sanctioned and seriously warned already. Any more silly behaviour on my part would send me flying out of the Toubaabys's residence for good. Monsieur has warned me that there are millions of potential houseboys out there just waiting for him to beckon."

He emptied the bottle into his glass to indicate his readiness to go away after answering the question Dieumerci was about to ask. He took a gulp, belched, and thanked everyone for the good and jolly company. Then he waited for Dieumerci to ask his question.

"I would like to know if your father was ever in Muzunguland, during his long and tortuous career as a Muzungulander soldier," Dieumerci asked Dieudonné, who was making no effort to subdue yet another yawn.

"Is that all you wanted to ask?" Dieudonné joked. "My father was one of the very first soldiers en Afrique noire to fight for Muzunguland," he told Dieumerci. "He was in Muzunguland for three years, where he was trained and qualified as a soldier. From Muzunguland, he returned to Muzungu-Avenir to defend the Muzungulander Empire. I remember all this very well. While my father was undergoing military training in Muzunguland, news used to reach us back home that he was a 'soldier at home'. But I knew that the Muzungulanders knew his home was not in Muzunguland, and that they wouldn't rest till he was back in Warzone, were their wars to spare his life. Up to this day, I still don't know what the bearers of the tidings in those days meant. Just like Muzunguland was made to pass for home for which Africans were called upon to spill blood and die in honour of, so were its African soldiers known as 'Les Combatants', and would retire, for those lucky enough, into the status of 'Les Anciens Combatants' to spend what was left of life fighting as 'Les Tirailleurs' for benefits from a reluctant Muzunguland." Dieudonné sighed, then exclaimed: "Qu'on nous tue, mais on ne nous déshonore pas quand-même!" And to imagine that today the Muzungulanders dare say of African immigrants – 'sans papiers' as they call them: 'Il faut que le Muzunguland cesse d'être le dépotoir de toutes les misères du monde! Immigration choisie, pas subie !' What ingratitude!" he spat. "Whatever happened to the *Liberté – Egalité – Fraternité*, in defence of which my father and the fathers of others were slaughtered?"

After calming himself a little, Dieudonné continued. "As I told you, he died shortly after my departure from home. He died fighting for Muzunguland, the Muzunguland that would not let a man who had lost his limbs fighting its wars to die a death of peace. Despite Muzunguland's beastlike callousness, after my father's death, the Muzungulander colonial administration deliberately created a problem about the allowances and pension that were his due as a soldier. They refused to pay the money to my mother, saying that they needed nobody else's signature but mine. I was the son, his heir, they said, as if they had sought my opinion before taxing him to death at their battlefronts. I refused to go home for that. I was determined to spend double the fifteen years that my father had spent fighting wars about which he knew so little. I didn't go back home because I believed that if the Muzungulanders were really honest with themselves, if they had a conscience, they didn't have to wait for me to sign before they could pay my mother the money. So I allowed all in the hands of Allah the Almighty, who brought me to Mimboland and who knows where and when I move to next. Remember that I neither ran away from home nor knew where I was heading when I left. Allah for sure was directing every step I took. And so long as Allah the Almighty is still up above, I am waiting down below." He pointed up and down with his forefinger to emphasise his point.

"But I don't see why the Muzungulander authorities refused to pay my late father's hard-earned money to my mother, his rightful wife. They said they wanted me, and me alone to sign. 'We cannot shave your head in your absence,' was their message to me. How absurd! Without my mother, could I exist? Suppose my father didn't have a son like me, does it mean he would never have earned money as a soldier fighting for Muzunguland? And if I really mattered to them that much, why hadn't they sought my opinion before amputating my father to death with their sterile wars? Imagine the audacity with which they had summoned my father to exile his humanity: 'We cannot shy away from necessary wars merely because cowards like you can't stand the sight of human blood', they had reprimanded, dragging him along. These are the type of things that make me weep, and marvel helplessly at our world and its contradictions. When I finally go home, Insha'Allah, – I would inquire from the king who ordered my father to join the Muzungulander army. If he, too, has died, his successor, I think, would have to furnish me with the information I need. But if he claims to know nothing about wars that were fought a long time ago, I would inquire at the offices of 'Les Anciens Combatants'." He paused, and for a moment seemed lost in thought.

Suddenly but calmly, he started speaking again.

"What gives me a little consolation is the thought that my mother is at home with villagers who have a high sense of hospitality and solidarity. They can't see her dying of famine and refuse to share with her the little they've got. Her situation isn't like mine here in the city where I'm suffering, though I work and strain like an ass." He tried to purge a haunting sense of guilt. How could he admit that he had acted irresponsibly, like a spineless young man? Running away from home the way he did was downright irresponsible, but he wouldn't admit it. It wasn't easy convincing his conscience, which is why it had tortured him since he left home. For long, he had refused to entertain the thought that his mother might be dead, which could only be a coping strategy, as it was clearly too much of a miracle to expect about a woman who was already in her fifties when he left Warzone over forty years back.

"All is in the hands of Allah the Almighty who is above and who oversees everything here on earth," he continued. More realistically, and for the first time ever, he added: "Perhaps my mother and sisters have died already. With the war raging between Musa and Hassan – contenders for the headship of Warzone– how can I be sure they live? Maybe they died long ago. Or maybe they are alive as refugees somewhere. How can I know? How do I find out when my homeland is ablaze fuelled by greed?" There was always a reason for inertia.

"If dead, they are much happier where they are. Better than living in this world of fear and uncertainty," he consoled himself.

Dieudonné was getting more and more hysterical, and his voice struggling with too much emotion.

"Again, instead of bringing about peace, Muzunguland and Greenbook Republic are stoking the flames of war. What can I do? All is in the hands of Allah above who knows everything."

At this point, Dieudonné started to sob. Tears formed and streamed down his cheeks like a bleeding wound. Then he broke down and wept like a baby, and everyone was stunned and filled with pity for him. Like Dieumerci, the others were equally amazed at how close the friendship between happiness and sadness was in this man from Warzone. At one moment, he could be cheerful and happy, and the very next he would be depressed, unhappy and all tears. It looked as if with him, happiness had its sad face and sadness its happy face.

Dieudonné wept inconsolably for about ten minutes, then he wiped his eyes with the back of his right hand, saying: "Allah be praised."

Dieumerci, who was particularly perplexed, thought it best to lead him home, especially as more and more people were coming into the Grand Canari for their evening drinking and dancing. So Dieudonné and Dieumerci bid everyone goodbye, and thanked Chopngomna, the generous supplier, and his friends in particular for the good time they had had together.

Dieudonné was drunk and Dieumerci was aware of it. With all care and concern, Dieumerci finally escorted him to the house where he soon fell asleep. Dieumerci stayed until Dieudonné started to snore and groan. Then he tiptoed out of the room, closing the fragile wooden door behind him. Even with the door closed, he could still perceive Dieudonné on the bed through the large holes on the walls. He hurried up back to the road and caught a panting bus for Chateau d'eau d'Assieyam where he lived.

CHAPTER FOURTEEN

Dieumerci rang at the gate. It was 9.30 a.m. The Guinness that he took the day before had made him oversleep. Or was it the football match he had played earlier in the day during which he had been so dehydrated that he stuck out his tongue whenever he saw sweat on the face of someone nearby? Perhaps both, as the dehydration had offered him a perfect excuse to indulge. He had been invited to play by a neighbour and student of the sports institute, the school for those whose heads were in their muscles. The match had taken place on a field constructed for the poor boys of Swine Quarter by the prolific Petit Pele, the one and only soccer legend of Mimboland, with money earned from advertising for the biggest sweet company – Sweet-Mimbo. A big billboard of Petit Pele holding out sweets to a group of ghetto kids had been deformed from: 'Petit Pele, qu'est-ce qui vous donne le goût des buts? Sweet-Mimbo bien sur!' to: 'Petit Pele, qu'est-ce qui vous arrache les dents? Sweet-Mimbo bien sur!' And his teeth had been blackened out to conform to the new meaning. After the game which Dieumerci's team had won, he had been persuaded by his neighbour to a celebratory bottle or two in luring company. And they must have overindulged, as he returned home late, barely sober enough to find his way to bed.

He remembered one thing though, clearly. He had even dreamt of Precious, the shapely, slim dark-skinned bar beauty with whom he had flirted more than once but whom he hadn't had the courage yet to say what he felt about her. It was a curious dream. Precious had sent him a postcard through Dieudonné with the following words: 'Hi Dear, hope you're doing great. I was very pleased to see you at the Grand Canari. You know what? Bizarre. I had you in my dream. We were having some snap shots in Muzunguland where we were visiting, and you came so close to me that I was tempted to send my hand around your waist and felt this tingling feeling. Your waist was very hairy. But how true is this? It's just a dream! It's supposed to be personal, but I decided to share it with you. I hope you don't mind it. Love specially prepared, preserved and reserved for you. Precious.' Strange thing, dreams.

Right now his thoughts were on Dieudonné, how he wept at the Grand Canari. Such tears captured his long tale of gloom perfectly, and in some instances, better than the words he had used. It was in this light that Dieumerci chose to understand Dieudonné's penchant for alcohol. Hence his conviction that Dieudonné would not be the drunk that he was had things at least gone the way his father had planned and hoped. Circumstances had forced Dieudonné to abandon his strong religious taboo against alcohol. From whatever angle that he examined the issue, Dieumerci saw that Muzunguland was mainly to blame for Dieudonné's misfortunes. The Muzungulander had made life impossible to his village community with the imposition of cotton farming, had forced his father into their army and taxed him to death with futile wars, had rendered him useless as a husband, ultimately forcing his wife – Fatimata and also eventually Tsanga – to abandon him, and had pushed him into exile, away from his loved ones, his mother and sisters, whose whereabouts he couldn't say. And, as if to kill him off completely, a Muzungulander lady employer and her priest had conspired to baptise him 'God's Gift'. Muzunguland and the Muzungulander had cursed Dieudonné. That was how Dieumerci saw things, in black and white, and with hardly the nuances of real life. Others, the Toubaabys included, were most likely to see the nuances – the eternal beauty and attractions of Muzunguland and the Muzungulander, for example, which unfortunately neither Dieumerci nor Dieudonné could capture even at the best of times.

If only he knew what even Dieudonné did not know – that Tsanga, upon leaving Dieudonné that fateful day, had struck the jackpot, relatively speaking and strictly by the standards of Swine Quarter, by falling into the hands of and eventually in love with a Muzungulander (albeit a rather localised, ordinary and used variant of the real thing with little to show in terms of the joys of superiority) – Dieumerci would have pierced the skies with his spear of conspiracy theories. Tsanga had found success in failure, because of her conviction that love knows no borders, pleased to move on from Dieudonné who had debased her to a dish best enjoyed only when drunk. She must have told herself, "Such an experience never again!"

And if Dieumerci were to listen to Monsieur Nupieds, an ex-convict, selectively recount his experiences with Mimboland and the Mimbolander the same way that he had recounted to Tsanga to win her heart, he wouldn't be that sweeping in his criticisms of Muzunguland and the Muzungulander. He would have been led to believe that the deviousness of his native Mimboland had frustrated many a Muzungulander and their dreams, leaving some like Monsieur Nupieds, unable to return home, because they were too ashamed for having nothing to show for years of fortune hunting. Monsieur Nupieds had come to Mimboland with money enough, had set up a bakery that had done well, given the Mimbolander love for Muzunguland bread, cakes and biscuits. But his sun had set when the greed in him had matured, and he had bought into the fake investment opportunities daily paraded by Mimbolanders rendered idle and crooked by too much or too little education. He had lost all his money in taxes and such fake deals, had been 'falsely' imprisoned for fraud, and had actually been on the brink of suicide when an urgent call came through to the maximum security prison from the Muzunguland Embassy in Nyamandem, asking him if he could be of service. "A man is not a man without his gun," Monsieur Nupieds reassured the

Muzunguland Embassy. Armed with physical strength enough to permit him to live his life without his head, Monsieur Nupieds snatched the opportunity and within hours was at the central train station, two AK-47 Kalashnikov assault rifles strung across the shoulders, waiting to catch the train heading north to Warzone. He was excitedly whispering his favourite tune, *The Spirit of Africa*, which a fellow Muzungulander prisoner had composed to keep alive his African dream:

> 'It lingers in your heart
> In your memories
> And in your taste buds
> The Spirit of Africa
>
> Touch it
> Feel it
> Savour it
> Taste it
> The Spirit of Africa
>
> Africa is:
> Exotic
> Natural
> Sensuous
> Unforgettable
> The Spirit of Africa
>
> Nurtured by Nature
> Matured with time
> Crafted into the perfect gift
> The Spirit of Africa
>
> Africa my dream
> Africa my love

Africa my diamond
Africa of riches
Africa of wars
Bullets forever
Ballots never
Afritatata…
Afritatata…'

Like Dieudonné, Dieumerci didn't know of Tsanga's chanced meeting with Monsieur Nupieds at the central train station of Nyamandem. Neither did he know of his success in convincing her to accompany him to Warzone where he was heading to take up a lucrative appointment as a mercenary for a pro-Muzunguland warring lord determined to have the last word over battles to secure the right to control the enormous deposits of black gold. No wonder both of them were not in a position to purge themselves of the stereotypes they had internalised of Muzunguland and the Muzungulander. And they therefore kept on hoping that some day Tsanga would somehow show up again at the Grand Canari, and life would return to normal – by Dieudonné's standards.

As Dieumerci waited for the Toubaabys to let him in, he tried to think of the best way he could help Dieudonné. He felt it was his place to do something to lighten the burdens of the old man, an attitude that came naturally to him. 'Be kind even to strangers, for everyone you meet in life is fighting some kind of battle.' He had grown up internalising these words, and now was the time to practise them. He thought of what he could do to show Dieudonné that he loved and respected him in the same way that he did his own father. One didn't necessarily need to have children of one's own to be respected by the young. Equally, a well-brought up child instinctively knew that everyone in the father's age group needed the same respect and love. Dieumerci was convinced that this attitude, which was quite prevalent, partly explained why in his home village everyone's business was the other's concern. The love and desire to live together as one people with the same aspirations for the common good was very strong. Reflecting on Dieudonné's life story, the cultural differences between Dieudonné and the Toubaabys were quite clear. In the culture of the Toubaabys, the motto was: Everyone for themselves and God for us all. Everyone tended to go their own way and hated interference of any kind, be this by government, family, friends or foe. The natural thing to do, it would seem, was outgrowing relationships, and if involved at all, to keep commitments at as elementary a level as possible, so that the severing of links remains an instant possibility.

"Perhaps this explains why they like fighting so many wars, why they co-opt others to fight their battles for them, and why they are never at peace with those in love with peace." The more Dieumerci thought about this, the more he felt sorry for Dieudonné, and the greater his urge to help him in whatever way possible.

He made up his mind to give Dieudonné two of his shirts. Being more or less of the same size despite their difference in height, he was sure his shirts would fit Dieudonné perfectly. But there was an issue, which Dieumerci considered even more important. It was the problem of how he could help Dieudonné return to his homeland to reunite with his family and people, or at least to know what had become of them.

If only because Dieudonné had been out of his village and country for ages, it was necessary for him to return and find out whether his mother and sisters were still alive, or whether they had fuelled the hungry flames of war. To Dieumerci, Dieudonné's rightful place was in his homeland, not in Mimboland. Dieudonné ought to go home, even if only to mourn for his family. He was convinced that a man who died in bed at the home where his umbilical cord was buried died a better death than those who passed away in a foreign land. Dieudonné had to return to Warzone despite the war that raged there. Dieumerci felt that it was possible for Dieudonné to die in peace at home, if only because a foreign land was never the place to die, let alone dying in peace. So he resolved to discuss the issue with Dieudonné.

Madame Toubaaby came to open the gate. She first looked through a spy-hole before doing so. When she opened the gate, Dieumerci greeted her.

"Bonjour, Dieumerci," she answered. "I have the habit of looking through the spy-hole to identify the visitor," she explained. "It helps to choose between the people I want to welcome and those I want to have nothing to do with," she added.

Dieumerci found her idea funny, so he asked, "What do you tell the visitor you don't want?"

Madame Toubaaby laughed.

"Your question is silly, isn't it?" she asked. Not expecting an answer, she went on. "It's silly. C'est bête! Ce que tu dis. Bête! This is my residence, isn't it? I have the right to act the way I like in my own home, don't I? If I don't want a particular visitor, I have to tell that visitor so in black and white, isn't it? I send away all visitors for my husband whom he hasn't told me about. If I admit you, it's because my husband has told me of you, isn't it? I like it that way. It keeps thieves and nuisances away, doesn't it? Also, this country breeds an awful lot of chronic visitors, popping in without invitation. I hate people who stick their heads through the gate and say: 'I was just passing by and wondered if you were in ...' Keep wondering, I tell them. The problem is that if we encourage people to visit when they aren't invited, they soon begin to stick around our house like mosquitoes, ready to suck and contaminate our blood, isn't it?"

Dieumerci was really amused by Madame Toubaaby's mannerism, though he did not dare to chuckle. He was not unaware of the damage that a silly giggle could cause. He wondered, however, why she made such an abusive use of 'isn't it?' No doubt the Muzungulander 'n'est-ce pas?' was at the heart of her corrupted Tougalish.

"Yes," admitted Dieumerci, "you may be right, Madame, but I find it difficult to see with you. I've been brought up in a home where it is an abomination to discriminate between visitors, or to build a fence round the compound to keep out visitors. We have been cultivated to receive everybody that calls, and to keep our doors wide open both to people we know and people we do not know. The very way in which our compounds are constructed facilitates our open-door approach to people, family and strangers alike. There are no fences round our houses, for instance, and everyone is free to come and go as they wish." Dieumerci sounded superior.

Madame Toubaaby smiled mockingly. Dieumerci hated the expression on her face and disliked to think that she thought of him as a narrow-minded, ignorant bush African. She made to answer him, and what she said proved him right.

"But that is normal in your tribe, isn't it?" said she, scrutinising him. "You are an individual and I'm another, isn't it?" She wondered if Dieumerci had imbibed enough Cartesian rationalism to temper his highly emotive personality and native customs. She would have to advise Monsieur Toubaaby to intensify his efforts at moulding him into a man of logic, and put an end to the primitive superstitious animal. She might have to start the instructing herself.

"Dieumerci," she called, "don't you think that the fact that you are black and I'm white, and that we each come from different cultures, is enough to make us think, act and do things differently?"

"Yes, that I understand, Madame," Dieumerci replied. "But we are all human beings, created by the same supreme God in his image, having the same soul. Our soul is neither Muzungulander nor Mimbolander, black nor white. At least the Bible says so." He was firm and confident about his point.

Madame Toubaaby's reaction was instant, and her disapproval of his line of argument total. "Never mind the Bible!" she screamed.

"I don't like arguments based on God, the soul and the Bible. They are luxuries I can't afford," she laughed. "I think you ought to know that I believe neither in the Bible nor in God. God doesn't exist. The Bible is a storybook like any other, and a very poor one at that, I must confess. Behaviour, far from being determined by God, is conditioned by one's nature and milieu. All those who believe in God are imprisoned by their fears and superstitions. And what they desperately need is self-liberation, open-mindedness and realism. To believe in God or the Bible is to seem to think that there is only one way of being happy. But I realised while still a teenager that there are as many ways of seeing and doing as there are individuals and societies seeking meaning. The believer in God who wants every other person to follow his footpath is totalitarian, blinded to the idea of basic human differences in tastes and tendencies, and has given up the struggle for meaning."

For a brief while, Dieumerci was confused. He didn't know what to say to keep the interesting discussion afloat. He was perplexed, quite confounded by what Madame Toubaaby had told him. How could a white person deny God's existence, yet Europeans forced Africans to adopt the Muzungulander's God and all he stood for? How could the very people who preached salvation and heavenly glories everywhere suddenly abandon their converts with the abomination they had authored? Why did Madame Toubaaby speak as if Africans had gone out of their way to bargain for God and the Bible? Could she have forgotten already how her forefathers had forced Africans to forgive and forget their atrocities in the name of the God of Christianity? A God whom they had rendered white in every sense? How could they turn around to behave as though they hadn't used the idea of 'Heaven' and 'Hell' to whip alternative modes of existence into a ridiculous defensiveness? Why had Christianity suddenly ceased to be glorious, grandiose and blissful? And what in her view had replaced it – consumerism? The more he contemplated this issue, the more he realised there was a lot to talk about.

"Please, Madame," Dieumerci started politely. "To Christians, we know that the Bible is regarded as the handbook of morality. It prescribes how Christians should live and let live. The same is true of Muslims and their Koran. What I want to know is how persons without religion distinguish between moral uprightness and decadence."

Dieumerci was pleased with the way he had made his point. He couldn't have made it any better. There was no doubt in his mind that he had forced Madame Toubaaby onto the defensive, where all she had to do was admit his victory and re-examine her defective philosophy of life. But he was mistaken.

Madame Toubaaby wasn't the type of person he could easily pocket, and he should have known better.

She couldn't help laughing mockingly again. It appeared as if starting each response with a cynical laugh was an established tradition of hers, just as was her meal of 'isn't it?' Dieumerci felt rather annoyed at her tendency to laugh off ideas that had taken him long to conceive and articulate.

"I'm happy you are reading broadly, Dieumerci," Madame Toubaaby commended. "*Philosophia Perennis* would help relax the tight-fitting screws of your mind, to make it more flexible and tolerant to other people, other ways and other ideas, isn't it? You just might come to understand that God, far from being a living entity, is a mere idea in the minds of those who believe in him, isn't it? An idea which when generally recognised the way you so-called Christians do, assumes a form of meta-existence that superimposes itself on the community of Christians, isn't it? But what gives an individual a sense of right and wrong isn't the idea or a book on this idea. Rather, it's the community of Christians that you as an individual are an integral part of, isn't it? To live together, interrelate and interact, people feel the need to sacrifice some of their identities in favour of common values, isn't it? Whenever one does this, and respects the rules that ensue, one is said to have *une conscience collective*, to be morally upright, *en d'autres termes*. But if one does otherwise, the contrary is true. Do you understand? I'm not too high for you, isn't it?" she concluded by switching on her detestable smile. Then she murmured to herself, "What on earth has my husband been teaching you students in Ethnologie?"

"Yes, I understand you, Madame," replied Dieumerci, forcing a smile of his own. If that is what knowledge means, ignorance is bliss, he concluded. "Does Monsieur Toubaaby have similar views on God?" he asked.

"That's a question for Monsieur Toubaaby to answer. I know what concerns me only. Ask of Caesar what is Caesar's," she parodied with a dubious laugh. "Isn't that what the Bible says?" she sounded too tongue-in-cheek for his liking.

"Where is Monsieur, Madame?" asked Dieumerci, with the timorous respectfulness of the primitive villager he had just been reminded he still was. He tried to hide the fact that he was displeased with Madame's attitude.

"He's gone to fetch Dieudonné, whom we want urgently," she told him. "There's a lot of work for him to do around here, because we're receiving some friends tonight."

"I'm facing some difficulties with the book I'm reading at present. So I want Monsieur to clarify a few issues in it."

"You could read something else while waiting for Monsieur to return. But I'm afraid your reading place in the store has been taken by one of my students at the university, who has come to consult some of my books. She will not be here for long anyway, so you could read in our sitting room in the meantime. You would have used the dining table but since we breakfasted, Dieudonné hasn't been around to clear the table. And I can't do it in his place. He is paid for it, isn't it?"

"Can I do it?" asked Dieumerci.

"Why do it?" retorted Madame Toubaaby. "Is it your job?" She gazed at him. "I have no money to waste on a houseboy who isn't at work on time, isn't it?"

"Madame, there's something I've always wanted to ask you," began Dieumerci, rather abruptly, "I would like to know why you have sent all your children back to Muzunguland. Does it mean that Mimboland isn't so good a place for them to grow up?" Dieumerci pretended he had forgotten what Dieudonné told them – that the Toubaabys had no children.

"What children do you mean?" Madame Toubaaby asked, baffled.

"I mean yours, Madame."

"Mine? Who told you I have children?"

"No one did, but I just thought ..."

"Just thought?" Madame interrupted. "Just thought? Why should you just think?" She gazed at Dieumerci, who mistakenly thought her to be angry.

"Forgive me for ..." Dieumerci tried to apologise.

"Why do you ask for forgiveness, Dieumerci? What have you done wrong? Nothing, isn't it? You are funny, isn't it? What I mean is simply that you shouldn't presuppose anything. Presuppositions aren't good, isn't it? I would prefer that you ask me any question that bothers you, and I'll answer it if I can. It's better that way, isn't it? If you are really interested to know, I don't have children, and the reason is simple. The world is overpopulated. There are too many mouths to feed and too little food. And we believe that we can best contribute towards better standards of life in the Third World, especially, if we do not help in making matters worse by procreating ourselves. You understand, isn't it?"

For a moment, Dieumerci wondered if it wouldn't be a good idea for Madame Toubaaby to consult her psychiatrist about her bouts of 'isn't its?'. He saw this as an illness like any other. How did others cope with her, when she was that monotonous and laughable? What use were bright ideas compromised by disgusting mannerisms? Dieumerci congratulated himself for the effort he was making not to giggle while Madame Toubaaby had her tantrums of 'isn't its?'.

"Yes, I do." Dieumerci replied, with little enthusiasm. Apart from the fact that he didn't understand how Madame Toubaaby's decision not to bear children should contribute to solving famine in the Third World, Dieumerci was very disgusted with her ideas. Her thoughts were strange and frightful. If her parents had thought in the same way as she, where would she have come from, to harbour such outrageous ideas about not bearing children? Dieumerci almost hated her for that. Unwilling to discuss anything with her further, he asked to be allowed into their luxurious sitting room where he sat to read.

CHAPTER FIFTEEN

Monsieur Toubaaby rang at the gate at 10 o'clock. His wife opened for him. He drove in and parked the car in the garage at the east end of the main house. He was alone and looked angry.

"You didn't bring him, n'est-ce pas?" Madame Toubaaby asked her husband as they both walked into the sitting room after performing the ritual of kissing and exchanging wristwatches.

"I found the mad idiot dead-drunk, unable to get out of bed even. I was so furious that I fired him there and then. He complained that he is forsaken without a job, and without money to pay his way back home. But who cares? That's entirely his problem." Monsieur Toubaaby was rattled, so was his Muzungulandish.

"You did well to dismiss him, n'est-ce pas? It's been too much, n'est-ce pas? We will have to get another houseboy as soon as we can, n'est-ce pas? But how do we solve tonight's problem? We definitely have too much work on our hands, n'est-ce pas?" Madame Toubaaby was as monotonous in her mother tongue as she was in Tougalish. But unlike in Muzungulandish where the 'n'est-ce pas?' wasn't always to be taken as a question, the 'isn't it?' in Tougalish wasn't as flexible as she thought it to be. Her literal translation didn't do her any good, yet she couldn't stop it because of the peculiar manner in which she employed her 'n'est-ce pas?'

"That's a serious problem that needs an urgent solution," said Monsieur Toubaaby, scrutinising his glasses. "But I haven't thought of one yet. I was so angry with that fool that I hardly stopped to think." He had the tip of the frame of his glasses between his lips and the keys of the car in his left hand. He was thinking of how the problem could be solved.

"What about Dieumerci?" Madame Toubaaby suggested in Tougalish, turning to face the latter. "Do you think he can help in any way?" she asked her husband, instead of seeking Dieumerci's opinion directly as an individual, in accordance with her earlier prescription.

It was then that Monsieur Toubaaby became aware of his student, who pretended to focus on his reading. He turned round and smiled his greeting to Dieumerci, who returned the compliment.

"Will you stay behind this afternoon to help us cook for our guests?" Monsieur Toubaaby enquired, peering into his eyes.

There was nothing Dieumerci thought to be as impolite as to look directly into someone's face when speaking to that person. His parents had always said so, and he had grown up with this belief that those who looked into his eyes when addressing him definitely had something they were trying to hide by faking braveness. But Dieumerci couldn't understand what Monsieur and Madame Toubaaby could possibly be hiding from him since they never stopped gazing into his eyes. Could the Toubaabys be criminals? Could they be afraid he might uncover who they truly were and alert the police? He wasn't sure, that couldn't be. The couple were just too rich to be involved in petty matters of city crime. The police were certainly beneath them. Maybe, as Madame Toubaaby had said earlier, Muzungulander culture expected the Muzungulander to behave differently. Maybe in Muzunguland, it would be impolite and suspicious not to glue your eyes on the person you are speaking to. 'What a strange place Muzunguland must be!' Dieumerci thought before replying to Monsieur Toubaaby's request.

"I don't know how to cook much, but if you gave me the necessary instructions on how to go about what, I could help," said Dieumerci with modest sincerity.

"No, that shouldn't be a problem, isn't it?" said Madame Toubaaby. "All the food has clear instructions written in black and white, to be followed. "We also need your services as a steward tonight. You don't mind, isn't it?"

"No, Madame, I don't mind," replied Dieumerci, cautiously amused by her ludicrous mannerism.

"How much do you think that we should pay you," inquired Monsieur Toubaaby, looking into Dieumerci's eyes.

"No, nothing. Why pay me? I'm helping you as a friend, am I not?" Dieumerci was quite shocked by the suggestion of being paid by someone he considered himself to be helping out as a friend.

"But you're making a sacrifice Dieumerci, for which you normally have to be rewarded. If you don't know how much we should pay for your services, I'd have to discuss it with my wife, based on what you actually do. But you can't refuse to be paid. That's the way we do it. It's our custom to pay for services." Monsieur Toubaaby was insistent.

"But it is my custom not to accept to be paid. I'm brought up to privilege relationships in the long term over instant material benefits. And I see much sense in this. If I don't expect to be paid back instantly for services rendered, then I have an interest in maintaining enduring relations with others, don't I?" Dieumerci couldn't see himself accepting to be paid. He wanted to be seen and treated as a friend, and not simply as someone hired, paid and fired. He detested the mercantilist opportunism and callous disregard for sociality implicit in such affirmations as: 'One good turn deserves another'; 'You scratch my back I scratch your back'; 'Everyone for himself and God for us all'; 'I'm not my brother's keeper'; 'Ours is a strictly employer-employee relationship'; and so on. Why this extreme fear to be socially indebted to one another?

Monsieur Toubaaby smiled knowingly. He was an ethnologist, a seasoned one.

Madame Toubaaby replied, "We know what your culture says, and we respect that. But you are at our home, where our culture applies. Our position is not negotiable, Dieumerci." She was firm.

Monsieur Toubaaby walked away.

Dieumerci knew that it was needless to insist further. It takes all sorts to make the world. He accepted to be paid, but decided not to keep the money for himself. He would give it to Dieudonné. Perhaps Dieudonné could survive on it until another job came his way. Dieumerci was also planning to help Dieudonné return to his native Warzone, though he didn't quite know how exactly he was going to go about it, or just how possible this was going to be. But there wasn't any crime in hoping.

CHAPTER SIXTEEN

Who said, 'He who is given to worries about the future can live through sufferings, torments and hazards of a lifetime in a single day or night of painful imagination'? Dieumerci found it hard to sleep. He turned from one side of the bed to the other, and did all his tricks, but just couldn't sleep. There was only one thing on his mind, a thing that made him restless, anxious like a child trying hard to please its foster parents. He was thinking of Dieudonné, of how he was going to make him happy.

Dieumerci turned over and lay on his stomach when his electronic watch chimed the hour of two in the morning. He was impatient with time on crutches. Why did this happen whenever he had a piece of good news to share? He could still recall how several years ago he had returned home from college with spectacular results but had had to wait infinitely for his father to return from his raffia bush. He had waited and waited the whole day, as it seemed his father might never return. Even the sun would not cooperate with him, staying defiantly at the same spot, blocking the way for evening to arrive, and for his father to share his news.

Indeed, Dieumerci was going through a similar experience. He had a piece of good news for Dieudonné, but it seemed the day might never break for him to make Dieudonné happy. If only he could fall asleep, time would pass much faster and he wouldn't have to wait for so long to go to Dieudonné. He wished for dawn, and prayed that nothing should befall Dieudonné before daybreak. He couldn't anticipate Dieudonné's reaction to the news. Would he scream with joy or would he attempt to jump up and shout his happiness? Would he laugh or would he, overcome with joy, cry instead? Would he celebrate his good fortune with a King Size, or would he sit down and be philosophical? What would his feelings be, to be working for a black master for the first time? Not just any black master for that, but a fellow Warzoner? A compatriot?

Dieumerci just couldn't wait to tell Dieudonné the good news. He could, even before telling Dieudonné anything, predict the latter's happiness and appreciation, once the news had settled in his stomach. Above all, Dieumerci was grateful for the opportunity he had had, much sooner than anticipated, to show his gratitude to Dieudonné in a significant way. If his mini-dissertation was going to be the masterpiece that he intended, it was thanks to the personal details with which Dieudonné had spiced up his analyses and interpretations.

Dieumerci was thankful for what had happened and wondered just how different things would have been had the Toubaabys not invited him to serve their guests that evening. Dieumerci couldn't but be grateful to God or Allah or Idea – as Madame Toubaaby would prefer.

Dieumerci turned round and lay on his back, pulled the blanket down with his feet, to cover himself properly, then tried to recollect the major events of the evening at the Toubaabys.

The first thing he remembered was himself in Dieudonné's white apron. His ridiculous reflection in the big mirror in the sitting room had made him laugh his heart out. He thought he looked so funny in the apron that he didn't understand why Monsieur and Madame Toubaaby, and their guests, weren't laughing all the time. Were they merely polite or had they no sense of humour? Anyway, that was that, as far as the apron was concerned. What he couldn't wait to see were the photos, which one of the guests had taken of him in the apron. What was the name again? He couldn't remember, only able to go as far as 'Louis–', though he knew for sure that the monsieur had a compound name, of which his beautiful middle-aged blond wife seemed quite fond. The monsieur was also an accomplished teller of jokes, a couple of which had stood out in Dieumerci's mind. One in particular had made everyone roar with laughter. It was the joke about a mad woman and a mad man at the city centre, where unattended refuse mountains had earned Nyamandem the title of 'La Ville Pourbelle – the most aromatised capital city in the world'. The mad woman took a look at the mad man, who was terribly filthy in his rags and flip-flops smeared with excrement – like a bed at the accident ward of l'Hôpital Général, spat in his direction and exclaimed: "It's people like you who give madness a bad name!" The mad man gazed back, a frozen smile of it-takes-one-to-tell-one on his bearded face thick with dirt, and asked: "Do you think my mother was a fool to give birth to a fool in 'le paradis de la folie'?" Then he walked away to a beckoning mountain range of garbage where thousands of flies, millions of maggots and hundreds of rats were scavenging for hidden treasures, screaming at the top of his voice: "Tant que Nyamandem respire, la pourbelle vie!"

It didn't take long for Dieumerci to get used to the cooking. All that was needed most of the time was for him to use his watch or the mighty clock that hung over the cooker in the kitchen. There were strange kinds of vegetables to boil briefly for ten minutes; ocean snails to grill at 120 degrees; soup to transfer from cans into a heated bowl; rice to boil in a programmed pot for ten minutes; and game to pressure cook for thirty minutes.

As the food was being cooked, Dieumerci was busy rehearsing what Madame Toubaaby had taught him earlier on setting the dining table. Afraid to make a mistake that might embarrass the guests, he got a piece of paper on which he wrote down the vital information. He remembered the crucial stages. It would be scandalous, Madame had told him, to serve 'le plat principal' before 'l'entrée', or to serve white wine with meat or red wine with snails, or something like that. It was a real ordeal, and he was happy to have done his best. At least, he had avoided giving the Toubaabys a major embarrassment.

The eating, when it finally began, was a major ceremony, a ritual in the true sense of the word. At times, Dieumerci couldn't help laughing. It was simply beyond his understanding why people had to make such a fuss about food. What did it matter if the red wine came in place of the white, or if someone chose to eat the bread at the end of the meal? Why was it obligatory to change the plates each time the guests were through with a particular course? Was it part of the process that the guests should eat so little? After the meal, when Dieumerci returned to the kitchen to do the washing up, he wondered if all this had been worth the trouble. The guests could have used a quarter of the plates and bowls that they had used, and might have done well with only a fifth of the quantity of food that he had taken the best part of the afternoon to cook. Was this all that it meant to be rich and famous? Or was it being civilised with a big C? It was nothing short of an extravagant waste in every sense, as far as he was concerned.

Even though the pets weren't directly invited to join the guests, Dieumerci was asked to prepare something special for them so that they too should feel the festivity. They ate long before the guests arrived, and Madame took the precaution to lock them up in their rooms, though they didn't particularly appreciate being caged. But Madame preferred this to people taking liberties with her cats and dog.

In the course of the meal, Dieumerci overheard a conversation between Monsieur Toubaaby and the only black guest present. It was something they said about Warzone that first attracted his attention. The more he listened to them, the more he became interested. Apparently, the tall, well-built, charcoal dark man, Mohammed, was a Warzoner, with a degree in nuclear physics from a prestigious Muzungulander university. He had just come from Muzunguland with a Muzungulander wife who was busy talking with Madame Toubaaby on myriad issues, including how to join the elite club of expatriate women in Mimboland. Unable to return to Warzone because of the raging civil war, Mohammed had applied for and got a teaching position with the University of Asieyam. He had just taken up duty and seemed to like it there, so he was going to settle, at least for a while, instead of going to work in Muzungu-Avenir, where he had had a more financially attractive offer.

Dieumerci had kept his ears pricked, catching what he could in between serving, and had heard many a weird joke, not least by Mohammed, who seemed to have a toilet sense of humour. His best jokes were about public toilets in Muzunguland and how he had become so fascinated with the graffiti on the walls of these toilets that he had become a compulsive visitor of them. At university, in bars, at railway and bus stations, he would find an excuse to use the toilet, and would pass from one to the other, noting down all the graffiti on the walls. Apparently, he was planning to write a book on graffiti in public toilets and was still waiting on his reluctant wife to join him in documenting the graffiti on women public toilets for comparative purposes. As if to make up for his frustration at not being able to visit women's public toilets, he had shared an inscription he had found at a male toilet in a very popular nightclub: 'In my next life, I'd like to be a toilet seat in the women's toilet.' From what Dieumerci had overheard, this book, if and when written, would definitely be a toilet bestseller. Dieumerci had retained only one of the graffiti, which he suspected might have been authored by Mohammed himself, a likely toilet cleaner or toilet seat in his student days in Muzunguland:

> 'Some come here to sit and think
> Some come here to shit and stink
> But I come here to scratch my balls
> And read the writing on the walls.'

Madame Toubaaby, at her jovial best, had volunteered a graffiti of her own, as if in an attempt to encourage Madame Mohammed to join the project: 'A bathroom with gold-plated taps is no place for you to be offloading second-hand water.'

Pleased with what he had heard, Dieumerci decided to meet Mohammed and his wife after their dinner, and to tell them about Dieudonné, a man with a worse fate than a public toilet in Nyamandem. But though he initially took for granted that being a Warzoner himself Mohammed couldn't sit by and watch another Warzoner suffer, Dieumerci found that Mohammed and his wife weren't easy to convince. They seemed reluctant to be seen to pull Dieudonné out of suffering prematurely. They wanted to know why Dieudonné had been fired by the Toubaabys, and what guarantee there was that he wasn't going to behave the same way with them. In the end, the best they could do was to give Dieumerci and Dieudonné a vague appointment for the following day. This, they were able to do only after the Toubaabys had told them that though a drunk, Dieudonné was good at house work when he came round to it. Mohammed and his wife could have him without reading too much into the fact that the Toubaabys had had enough of him. To his credit, Monsieur Toubaaby had said: "Dieudonné is certainly not the flimsiest fellow that we have ever seen."

Dieumerci turned round again and slept on his stomach. His watch chimed four, and he knew that he had two more hours to go. Thinking about the appointment with Mohammed, he felt the result was a foregone conclusion. He still couldn't see how Mohammed would let his fellow countryman starve. Meanwhile, he would give Dieudonné the MIM$2,000 the Toubaabys had offered him for his services. They had been overly generous to pay him so much for helping out for one evening, especially given that they paid Dieudonné only MIM$6,000 a month. Was it because Dieudonné attended mostly to their pets? Whatever the reason, he was pleased he had decided to give Dieudonné the money. With such an amount, Dieudonné could purchase something to eat and even to drink while things were being sorted out. Again, he closed his eyes and made an attempt to sleep. This time it worked.

CHAPTER SEVENTEEN

Tick … tick… tick … Dieumerci jumped up … stunned. He had overslept! The time was 10 o'clock. He rushed out of bed and out into the collective bathroom for a quick wash. Then he dressed up and hurried out, forgetting to think of breakfast. It was only when he was already in the bus for Swine Quarter that he realised how hungry he was. But there was no turning back. He would have to buy two loaves of bread along the way for himself and Dieudonné, who was likely to be hungrier. He would also take along a bottle of King Size just in case. 'Help others and others will help you,' he remembered his late mother's words, which he tried to keep as best he could.

Once at the Swine Quarter bus stop, Dieumerci alighted and went into a nearby store where he bought 'deux pains chargés avec pâté et sardines'. Then he proceeded to an off-licence bar further up the road to buy some beer. As he approached the bar, he saw a man wearing a T-shirt bearing the photo of President Longstay. The man was in conversation with the lady of the bar, who was dressed in the emblematic colours of the ruling party:

"Bonjour, Madame."

"Bonjour, Monsieur."

"It is hot this morning. One must cool down," said the man, empting beer bottles of their leftovers.

When there was nothing more to empty, the man walked away contented, a full bottle of assorted beers in hand.

"This man always shows up in the morning just before the beer distributors are here to pick up the bottles," the bar lady told Dieumerci, whose eyes followed the man round the corner.

"Is he normal?" Dieumerci asked with his eyes only.

"Yes, he very well is," said the lady. "At first I thought he was a little mad, but he looks quite stable."

Hoping his Dieudonné would never fall this low, Dieumerci paid for the beer, thanked the lady and left. Then he branched off from the main street into the bleeding ghetto and started to pick his way through muddy meanders of footpaths and shacks whose mud walls were delicately sustained by ant-infested wood. The general level of hygiene in this part of Nyamandem was below zero and Dieumerci's appetite fled because of the nasty sights he saw. He didn't know whom to blame for the indiscriminate disposal of human excrement, dog shit, and the colony of flies that exploited the situation, or the multitudes of rats and cockroaches that celebrated impunity.

Dieumerci doubted if Swine Quarter was the right place for these animals. If food and survival were what they sought, then exuberant Beverly Hills was the place to be, not destitute Swine Quarter. How could these rats and cockroaches remain in Swine Quarter where even humans were dying unattended? Why couldn't they migrate to Beverly Hills where there was food in abundance, and where eating was more of a ritual than a need? Just why did these animals stick around as if glued to destitution like the lives they plagued? Was the Bible serious when it predicted the poor would lose even the little they have to the rich? Was Dieumerci to believe that these rats, cockroaches, flies and mosquitoes were part of a conspiracy by the rich of Beverly Hills?

If Dieumerci could make the rats and cockroaches tell their story, they would have told him how hard they had tried to escape the poverty of Swine Quarter. Over the years, they had schemed and risked their lives to be allowed into Beverly Hills, had smuggled themselves along in the shopping bags, car booths, jacket pockets and other consumer gadgets of the rich, but each time the savage resolve against "unwanted aliens" had forced them back dead and alive. Entire families of rats, cockroaches, flies and mosquitoes had perished under the weight of the toxic chemicals of the exterminators employed by the rich to keep them out and dead. Beverly Hills, they would have told Dieumerci, was a no-go area for the likes of them, and had cultivated a shocking sense of impatience and double standards – using 'raticides' and insecticides to deny them visas and a right to life while at the same time throwing parties for stray cats and homeless dogs.

Dieumerci was so wrapped up in his thoughts that he didn't notice when he came to Dieudonné's shack. He was in fact bypassing the shack when Dieudonné, who was perching on his broken chair in front of the shack and weeping, recognised him.

"Dieumerci!" he exclaimed between sobs.

Dieumerci turned round, startled.

"Don't say you've forgotten about me already," said Dieudonné, disbelievingly. "Une méconnaissance inpardonable," he added, like a leaf off one of Monsieur Toubaaby's scholarly volumes.

"Oh, Dieudonné, it's you! I'm sorry," said Dieumerci, coming back with open arms to embrace the old man. "Don't weep," he reassured him. "One door closes, another opens," he took out his handkerchief and started wiping the tears from Dieudonné's eyes. "Can you imagine!" he exclaimed, putting down his little parcel and the bottle, after Dieudonné had stopped crying. "I was so deep in thought that I forgot to look up, and so didn't realise that I had reached where I was going."

"Do you mean you were actually coming here? To see me?" Dieudonné was still incredulous. "Do you actually mean that you weren't trying to avoid me?"

"Of course, not!" said Dieumerci, spreading a piece of paper on which to sit next to the old man. "Don't be silly, Dieudonné," he went on. "Such thoughts should never cross your mind," he said.

"Akwaba! Karibu! … Karibu!" Dieudonné shouted his welcome, relieved. "I know that I shouldn't think like that, but who ever behaves the way we expect them to behave?" asked

Dieudonné, his head turned contemplatively towards Dieumerci. "Who knows any more who is capable of what? Isn't ours a strange world?"

Dieudonné looked pale and frail, and Dieumerci was grateful to have thought of the sandwich. He could see that Dieudonné's thoughts were all on his woes. Tsanga had deserted him, he had been fired and there was little in his past to brighten his present.

"Could you have expected Monsieur and Madame Toubaaby to treat me the way they've done?" he asked Dieumerci, who shook his head in sympathy. "And if I can receive such treatment from people whom I've served for five years, how much more of a lad whom I met barely a few days back?"

Dieumerci was dismissive of Dieudonné's fears and mistrust, though he understood that anyone in Dieudonné's situation would have similar concerns. However, he was pleased that such misgivings and feelings of abandonment were soon to end. He unfolded the paper and took out the two loaves of bread. Dieudonné's eyes brightened and his countenance changed to accommodate the window of hope Dieumerci had opened. With his eyes he smiled 'Ahsante sana' and thanked Allah the Almighty even before a loaf was offered.

Dieudonné took a bite of the bread and asked for a glass of water. Dieumerci pointed at the bottle of King Size, but Dieudonné shook his head: "Water first," he said.

Dieumerci went into the shack and was soon back with water in a plastic bowl. Dieudonné drank and apologised for forgetting that Tsanga, his run-away wife, had taken both of their only glasses with her. The bowl Dieumerci used belonged to Dieudonné's complaining neighbour, Monsieur La Chance. Dieumerci told Dieudonné not to worry, and to eat his food in peace. Dieudonné was thankful as he bit, chewed and forced the sandwich down with water. Dieumerci watched him eat and was thankful that he hadn't come a minute too late.

When Dieudonné finished eating, Dieumerci took the second loaf into the shack, and suspended it on a long rope on the ceiling to keep it safe from the rats and cockroaches. Dieudonné would eat it again in the evening before packing out and going to live with Monsieur and Madame Mohammed, Insha'Allah. Hopeful though he was, Dieumerci once more summoned God to Dieudonné's aid to make Monsieur Mohammed realise how desperate his Warzoner compatriot was.

Dieudonné asked for the bottle to be opened, which Dieumerci did with his teeth in the absence of an opener. Before drinking from it, Dieudonné stood up, walked to the door and poured some of the beer on the threshold, saying: "To my late father and forefathers." Remarking that Dieumerci had noticed the tiny bit he poured, he added: "Just a bit of whisky is enough libation; too many libations make an ancestor drunk, and nobody would like to have an ancestor with a hangover – like all drunks, they get argumentative."

Dieumerci laughed. "Evil genius, you are," he told Dieudonné.

To describe Dieudonné as shocked and incredulous when Dieumerci presented him the money and told him of the job prospect would be to understate his reaction. Yet, there are no words to capture what took place. How can one describe the fact that Dieudonné was very apologetic, stalked by a feeling of guilt and shame, or that he wept his joy and gratitude, instead of jumping out of his two-legged chair to embrace a friend indeed? What words can most aptly capture and recount the fact that Dieudonné initially found his luck too good to be true, and thus initially declined to accompany Dieumerci to meet the Mohammeds?

CHAPTER EIGHTEEN

Today Dieudonné is still employed by Monsieur and Madame Mohammed. Whether or not he is treated better by his latest masters isn't the important question. What matters to him, more than everything else, is his beloved but embattled fatherland. Dieudonné wants to know when his homeland will be peaceful enough for him to return from exile. He is desperately looking forward to being laid to rest in the village where his umbilical cord was buried. He misses his home village to the point of tears, and although Mimboland has been more than generous with welcome, his heart has never really left home. The pain of having abandoned his family in search of what he knows not is acute. Unfortunately, Monsieur Mohammed his compatriot cannot help him, as he thinks of Muzunguland as home and talks of Warzone sparingly and disparagingly.

Dieudonné can't make sense of his boss's divorce with home despite his obvious abundance of means to visit as regularly as he likes. What original sin must Warzone have committed against Mohammed to deserve such oblivion? But he refuses the temptation to be judgemental, recalling his friend of late, Masa Chief Cook Godwill Kakakaka, who once said, 'We are so harsh on ourselves most of the time that we don't need it from other people.'

Life continues. Things have changed, less for the better than for the worse. Uncertainty has enshrined itself with shock and awe. Gone are the days when it was possible to dream of manna falling from the skies of Beverly Hills and beyond.

Dieudonné still visits the Grand Canari where he drinks, gets drunk and, to the rhythm of therapeutic music, dreams of home and of Tsanga's second coming. And the music is particularly helpful in the absence of any real will among the enabled to fish the disabled out of the miseries of indifference and indignity. Those charged with making life better have been raised with the ideals of making life impossible. They can't resist the temptation of keeping things the way things are. Gone are the days when the words, 'Those who make peaceful change impossible make violent change inevitable', used to chill many an elite spine with fear. Today, there is neither mobilisation nor the desire to mobilise as everyone who can is stunted by greed. There are lots of words and activity in the name of change for the better, but most of it is like cycling vigorously on the spot, with no real mileage to show. And, as the bandwagon of inequities and impunities magnets intellectuals, politicians and moral authorities to celebrate dissemblance and appetite, new tunes particularly intended to help ordinary folks subsist the crises are making their rounds in the bars that litter the land. As every crisis creates its opportunists, Madame Gazellia Mamelle, the proprietress of the Grand Canari has set up a permanent all-purpose, all-night, all-day band, and is cashing in on mass misery big time. And she is not alone.

Thank God for the conviviality of music in the company of the bottle.

Bikutsi, with its suggestive erotic and distinctive focus on wriggling to social commentary, frustrations, sex and relationships, and the private lives of prominent individuals into the public senses, has gained the most in popularity. Its message of hope and faith in traditional values and dignity has found suffrage among the sidestepped bulk of the ghettoes and beyond.

Particularly frail and finished though he might seem these days, with a good Bikutsi tune and a winning beer bottle cap to spur him, Dieudonné can't resist pounding the ground with his feet and shaking his body in trance-like frenzy. He, 'vieux capable', might not be capable any longer of the 'tremblement de terre' of youth, or even of the 'tremblement de fesses' that red hot music induces, but the music revives memories that have refused to fade with age. To him and others who worship at the Grand Canari, the therapy that Bikutsi brings is life-saving, trapped as they are in misery and the constant threat of death. It offers them an opportunity to scream with their feet: 'Devalue as you may, tax us into the depths of misery as you care, inflate prices to hit the skies, do whatever you please, we can walk on thorns, shoes or no shoes.' A new and popular cycling dance style, *Pédale*, has come with the born-again Bikutsi. At the Grand Canari, once a moving Bikutsi piece is played, dancers crush together on the circular floor at the centre of the gigantic wooden block, shaking in frenzied trances, intoxicated with physical and emotional pleasure, yearning to purge themselves of the frustrations of life at the margins. Under the threat of death induced by poverty, plagues, disasters and the indifference of those in positions to make a difference, the accelerated beat does the trick, and with each vibrant song, the accumulated uncertainties and insecurities seem to melt away, and are even forgotten, as Mimbolanders cycle away intensely. In this sense, *Pédale* is proving quite empowering as it offers the forgotten the chance to deride those who have made it a habit of poking fun at ordinary lives.

And the music, when not pregnant with questions beyond the indispensable technicians of state power to answer, is deliciously raw, meant as it is, to shock the dead and dying out of silence and compliance.

The most provocative singer to enter the scene in the neighbourhood of Swine Quarter is Precious, the creative, shapely, slim dark-skinned bar beauty Dieumerci had flirted with, dreamt about, and eventually fallen for. Having convinced herself that she needed a song to make it in life, she is determined to keep her song alive. Thanks to the all-purpose, all-day, all-night band at the Grand Canari, and thanks to Madame Gazellia Mamelle's nose for money, Precious has risen to ghetto stardom with 'Swine Quarter', her debut album, although she is yet to reap the financial benefits of being a star. But this does not stop Madame Gazellia Mamelle, her employer and manager, from laughing all the way to the bank, at least by the standards of the ghetto.

Precious the singer hunting for a breakthrough has caught both the nearest and the best among the clientele of Grand Canari. With a most amazing voice like a baby canary, she awakens the senses and gets people in the mood with her songs. She is simply sensational and with the confident, supportive and yet-to-find-a-job Dieumerci by her side, she faces the crowds without fear in her eyes. Even the rats, lizards and cockroaches on the rafters and in the crevices of Grand Canari seem to sing along when Precious appears on stage.

Dieudonné approves of Precious' relationship with his young friend but is uncomfortable with the sexually explicit nature of her music, which he can only stand when more than doctored by King Size. At Dieumerci's mini-dissertation defence where she insisted upon entertaining, Precious took the jury quite by storm with her suggestive voice and luring wriggles, bringing to the dance floor even the usually superior Monsieur Toubaaby and perhaps influencing in no small way the final decision to award a "mention très bien avec felicitation des danseurs". The president of the jury, a potbellied 'bon vivant' with sideburns, a thick moustache and sharp white eyes, had sent the hall roaring with laughter when he likened Dieumerci's mini-dissertation to Precious' mini-skirt: "A good mini-dissertation is like a mini-skirt," he laughed, "sufficiently short to arouse interest, but long enough to cover the subject." And with penetrating eyes, he had explored the contours of Precious' refined nose, and sampled her dimples, shapely hips and long trendy legs to prove his point. He had also imagined himself whispering triumphantly, "Slowly …

slowly. Je suis un cardiaque. Ne précipite pas ma mort, chérie…",
meaning, I am a heart patient. Don't rush my death, chérie…

This president of the jury disgusted Dieumerci in the same
way that President Longstay had when, asked by a female
Muzunguland journalist: 'Monsieur le President, what are
your thoughts on the Mimboland woman?' had replied: 'La
femme Mimbolandaise c'est un sujet sur lequel je m'ettends
longuement.' The Mimboland woman is a subject on which I
dwell at length. Were Dieumerci not at his mercy, he would
certainly have called the president of the jury to order when
the latter, in that ravenous voice of his to whom 'toute femme
est femme', whispered to Precious: "Your dimples are so deep
that my wallet can get buried in them any time anywhere."
Dieumerci could only hope the day would come when he could
edit the professor's lips from 'L'élève,' dit le professeur, 'est un
imbecile' to 'L'élève dit le professeur est un imbecile.' That is,
'The student,' said the teacher, 'is a fool.' to 'The student said
the teacher is a fool.'

When Dieudonné tells Precious to tone down on her
suggestive expressiveness, she says there is nothing to tone
down. "It's a generation thing," she laughs him off and by way of
making it up to him, asks Chantal the multipurpose new barmaid
to flood him with King Size. Careful not to give the old man a
heart attack of false hope, Precious and Dieumerci are secretly
saving away from the little she earns to pay Dieudonné's way
back to Warzone. They have also launched an extensive SOS
to reunite him with his beloved Tsanga, determined to make
it possible for both to undertake the journey of reconciliation
with his homeland. How they wish Dieudonné's other friends
and acquaintances could chip in. But not even Chopngomna has
been enthused to do more than help Dieudonné with just more
King Size.

Not knowing of the plan Precious and Dieumerci have put in place, life continues as normal for Dieudonné.

"Silly girl," Dieudonné will whisper in between gulps of the beer kindly offered by Precious. "I'm fond of her despite all. And what is more, she keeps my Dieumerci happy." She must be lying when she claims my young friend adores her because she is as tiny as a mosquito, Dieudonné would think, remembering her latest slogan with a laugh: "A moment on the lips, a lifetime on the hips." Then he would tell himself, "I'd rather go for the hips any time, anywhere," agreeing to differ. His thoughts would turn to his beloved Tsanga. "*Mi Yeewnii* Tsanga – 'missing you badly Tsanga'" he would add in his mother tongue, as if hoping to reach his ex-wife by telepathy. "Wherever she is, I'm warning every man to keep his hands off her. Ne la piratez pas. C'est ma femme."

What Dieumerci for sure has confessed he loves about Precious, that is, apart from her talent and flare for visibility, is to put it in his own words: "The fact that Precious, despite the call of the fame of the bar, has remained cool-headed and has kept her ebony dark complexion intact. You know, when you go to the restaurant and say you want 'omelette nature' – that is what she is. She has not diluted her looks and that is what is good about her. No wig, no bleaching creams, no screaming perfumes, no red-hot lipstick, nothing. Just her immaculate ebony dark, composed self."

The mention of 'restaurant' and 'omelette nature' any time, anywhere would remind Dieumerci of his first attempt to impress Precious following his dream of the romantic letter she sent him. He had eventually plucked courage and gone to Grand Canari to invite her out for a real meal at his favourite restaurant in Swine Quarter. Known as Social Eating House with the words 'No Credit Today – For Credit Come Tomorrow' inscribed firmly in bold above the menu, the restaurant was a modest shack. It was situated in the backyard of another bigger shack occupied by someone rather generous with her bathwater and overly proud of her dirty underwear, a fact not at all appreciated by clients with delicate constitutions, forced to enjoy their meal in the face of these sordid realities. Naturally, those with undemocratic stomachs threw up even when they would vouch that the food was delicious. The proprietress, although a superb cook of some of the best delicacies in Mimboland – such affordable foods as: Water Fufu and Eru, Kanda, Dry Fish and Red Meat; Pounded Cocoyam and Ndole; Fufu Corn and Vegetable; Gari and Okro Soup with Egusi; Achu and Meat, Towel, Bible, Exhaust Pipe and Roundabout; –ran the risk of being mistaken for running a food poisoning agency, just because of a neighbour who would neither dispose of her bathwater properly nor keep her dirty linen indoors despite the verdict of a million flies. The proprietress had threatened court action but the neighbour had in turn threatened her with witchcraft: "Un si minable restaurant. La cuisine de toute première qualité my head," she spat. "If you try, you shall see."

And with such language, the proprietress knew only too well not to dare. "Na black man be number one enemy for black man," she sighed, then added in Muzungulandish: "Le nègre mesure sa force contre la misère de son voisin."

So Precious had not been impressed. Although she had enjoyed the food and had thanked Dieumerci for a lovely meal, she had immediately thrown up in the open, seeing the filthy bathwater and stained underwear, and had been so sick that he had had to rush her first to a pharmacy, and then home where she, upon recovering, had asked him to prepare for her an 'omelette nature'.

Precious is known popularly as SIDA (salaire insuffisant difficilement acquis) among fans who are just as overworked and underpaid as her, and some of whom can't drink if they eat and can't eat if they drink because their salaries are just too low. She has endeared herself to 'ces privés des délices de la vie' – these deprived of the delights of life – with the wordings of her song on their desperate situation: 'Le Seigneur regarda notre travail et en fut content. Il vit notre salaire, se retourna et pleura amèrement, The Lord looked at our work and was pleased. He looked at our salary, turned around and cried bitterly.Particularly hard-hit are breadwinners who have become bread-losers and bread-beggars. 'Some days we have work, some days we don't; but the price of bread must always be met,' she sings, and they know that she knows where the shoe of life's uncertainties pinches them the most. Like all ordinary Mimbolanders in bleeding ghettoes like Swine Quarter, her fans have refused to give the powerful the pleasure of leading them away in handcuffs. They insist on their share of life's delights with such spontaneous exclamations as: 'Qu'ils ne nous tiennent pas par le ventre!' She has been branded "une fille dangereuse à suivre de prêt" by the ghetto media, because of the wordings of the two lead songs of her debut 'Swine Quarter' album subtitled: *Tremblement des Fesses*. The lead song, by which the poorly produced album is known, has been banned from national radio and television by the authorities (who adore the tune in the privacy of bars and nightclubs with the help of the bottle, if *radio trottoir* holds sway, and have been known to keep their mistresses busy with the new dimensions of resting inspired by Precious). This has only made her music more popular even among the high and mighty of Beverly Hills, who regularly use it at private parties and health fitness clubs that promise long life through 'le confort du sport'. Some among the high and mighty have cultivated such wild fantasies about her that she no longer answers her own mobile phone and is forced to change numbers every now and again. But it is the second song which Dieudonné can barely stand when drunk because of the poignancy of its message and also because of the phrases in Nkola that keep him hoping for a reunion with his beloved Tsanga. In the song, composed as a coded message to register her frustration with Dieumerci – 'le bonbon de mon coeur', who initially kept postponing the extravaganza of full contact with such infuriating questions as: 'Do you know the ex-boyfriend of your ex-boyfriend's ex-girlfriend?', a young woman in a letter to a male friend curiously named 'Monsieur Kondom', shares her experiences of the challenges of safe sex. Roughly translated from the intricate mixture of Nkola, Muzungulandish and Pidgin that is the song, the words would be:

"Dear Monsieur Kondom,
How well can we boast of condom usage?
Is the condom handy for other parts of the body
serviced by intimate contact?
How well can condoms resist long hours of intense activity?
Can condoms not be outgrown with familiarity?
Can a body burning with emotions control these things?
Shouldn't we just leave all in the hands of God?
He takes care of the poor and the helpless, doesn't He?
What is my condom-skipping fee?
I want my 'Omelette Nature'."

Even Madame Gazellia Mamelle, the sumptuous, amply endowed, bejewelled termite queen of the Grand Canari is known to wriggle to this song in the right company, inviting her doubly bubbly bulk to pay tribute to her new-look precious money-making machine. Rumoured to lure young men with enticements of cash, car and mobile phone, and to have a horsewhip to exact compliance in her bedroom, Madame Gazellia Mamelle has induced a young male journalist friend to publish praises about the 'Swine Quarter' album, and to do a video clip of her in sexy XL lingerie wriggling and screaming: "C'est le champion du monde, le zengé, le zanga, le quataquata, le super afobo, l'ultime zic-zic-zic, l'ambiance, le ndombolo nonstop, la total satisfaction, la sagacité des fesses, le passé marché partout, la mort subite! When you dance-am well well, na so you makandy di shake like say dem shock-am with electric. C'est un véritable festival des fesses, a real feast of the buttocks." And the teenage journalist knows exactly what she is talking about, Madame Gazellia Mamelle having compelled him to discover better than an idle fascination with the smaller the tighter, the tighter the sweeter. To feel the wisdom in the saying: 'Les vieilles marmites font des meilleurs plats'. He knows her bedroom inside out. It is there that she is most likely to call him " Myfavouritebra ", reading directly from a mighty poster on the wall behind the bed, if her goggles are nearby: 'A friend is like a good bra: hard to find, supportive, comfortable; always lifts you up, never lets you down or leaves you hanging, and is always close to your heart!'

Beyond him, Madame Gazellia Mamelle, who has the reputation of shrinking men with her eyes, prides herself with having in her an embedded antenna that makes her know the moment a boy is undressing her with his youthful looks.

"L'argent appel l'argent," Dieudonné affirms every so often. "Dieu est grand," he will whisper. "C'est vrai qu'il faut rever, mais il ne faut pas faire des rêves exaggerés." He knows only too well that life does not begin and end with the bottle, music and dance, however therapeutic or however much Madame Gazellia Mamelle would want it. So he remembers to tend his sheep, because today, unlike previously, he lives in the same compound as Monsieur and Madame Mohammed. They tolerate him to go out during his time off and to do as he likes, but within the strict confines of their expectations. Even when overcome by alcohol, as happens occasionally, Dieudonné is forced out of bed by an alarm clock designed for the truly deaf and brainless like Onguene, the sleeping night watchman at Monsieur and Madame

Toubaaby's. It rings – "rattles my senses like a mighty cock-a-doodle-doo!" – to tell him that it is not yet the final *uhuru* for the likes of him. The freedoms of the future are yet to be born.

Madame Mohammed must be pregnant. Not long ago, she returned from a meeting of the elite club of expatriate women with a notice advertising a 'wonder housekeeper-cum-nanny' by the name of Handie that left Dieudonné in no doubt. He overheard her reading it out to Monsieur Mohammed.

"What if Madame is not pregnant?" the thought crossed Dieudonné's mind. "What if the Mohammeds are thinking of passing me on? What notice would they pin up to attract offers – 'Dieudonné, smilingly yours'?" He feared, but sought to reassure himself. "It wouldn't be something I haven't seen before." He smiled with difficulty and shaking his head in resignation, added, "What is meant to be is meant to be."

As long as he is in service, breakfast for Monsieur and Madame, in sickness and in health. And more!

"Dieudonné! Have you cleaned the toilets yet?"

"I'm doing them, Madame."

"Have you sprayed the rooms and garden with insecticide?"

"Not yet, Madame."

"Hurry up! There is a lot to be done. My underwear is waiting, Monsieur's..."

"Yes, Madame." Dieudonné concurs. "Dreams are dreams, life is life," he whispers harmlessly. "Le dehors est dure, le dedans plus dure. The burdens of life are too heavy. On va faire comment? Masters. We are what they want us to be. The more I try and fail in my attempt to shape my life, the more I realise how my will is but a tiny little bit of Allah's grand design. Which is why I say 'Insha'Allah'. Dieu est grand. Man yi own na man yi own."

He is sad, deeply sad, but doggedly devoted.

"Ma vie ne vaut rien, mais rien ne vaut la vie," he tells himself more times a day than he can recollect.

Grand Canari beckons.

"They say nothing is impossible," Dieudonné murmurs between gulps. "But nothing will come of nothing. I am a nothing man. I live a nothing life. Just how can nothing be impossible?"

He gets up, takes a shaky step forward.

"De qui se moque t-on?" Dieudonné screams violently, warming up to the musical frenzy.

Precious is singing a song he adores: 'On ne meurt jamais deux fois.'

Dieudonné makes a commendable effort to dance and sing along: "'Ordinary people just want to be happy. All they want to do is to feel close to life once in a while ...'"

Precious winks at Dieudonné.

He winks back in recognition.

He is crying.

He is happy.

He is at Grand Canari.

And Dieumerci, as usual, gives him reason to keep hope alive with soothing words. "Those who say little things don't matter," he tells Dieudonné, "should know how the lion feels when a fly enters its nostrils."